SLOW DRINKERS,

GIANT BALLBAGS

&

SMELLY BASTARDS

A NOVEL

Matt Micros

"It is one of the blessings of old friends that you can afford to be stupid with them."

Ralph Waldo Emerson

Copyright 2017 Matt Micros
All rights reserved
ISBN-10: 996252-6-3-0
ISBN-13: 978-0-9962526-3-8

<u>*Also by Matt Micros*</u>

~Five Days~

~The Knights of Redemption~

~The Chameleon~

~The Greatest Mann in the World~

~Nick Nelson Was Here~

~The Music Box~

~Destinare~

TABLE OF CONTENTS

SLOW DRINKERS,
GIANT BALLBAGS
&
SMELLY BASTARDS

For old friends and a lifetime full of memories...

I THE END

Jim Reilly woke up dead and he was really pissed off about it. He snapped open the paper while sitting on the can, the way he did every morning, and found himself staring at an old picture of himself in the obituary section on Page 6. It wasn't even a good picture.

"Jim Reilly, 45, of Stratford, died suddenly yesterday of unknown causes. A lifelong sports enthusiast, Jim was a New York Mets season ticket holder for 15 years in the seats directly in front of Jerry Seinfeld's suite. They spoke five times during the games they attended together, but he believed they had an unspoken mutual admiration, even though there was no logical reason to believe that. Jim was a novelist in his free time, when he wasn't working for the Town of Stratford in their Park and Rec Department as a youth league coordinator. His books had sold a grand total of 42 copies, when he decided to take

matters into his own hands and buy a few hundred copies, which drove him high enough up the Amazon Best Seller Lists to get recognized by people who would not have otherwise seen him. The response was nothing short of amazing, as he went on to slowly grow a following that helped him sell two million copies over the next year. And yet, he never moved out of the small home he had shared with his wife of fifteen years, the pre-deceased, Sharon.

Jim believed in accountability instead of excuses, kicking off from the 25 yard line, paying people exactly what they were worth regardless of the demand, and he was vehemently opposed to baseball managers removing a good player from a game due to a righty-lefty match up. He also believed that he could do nearly any job in the country better than anyone who currently did them, and had no problem sharing his ideas with anyone who would listen--along with a few who would have preferred not to.

He is survived by a brother, Sam, whose whereabouts is unknown, and millions of fans spread around the globe, who are encouraged to attend the funeral service, as no one should be buried alone. In lieu of traditional calling hours, there will be an Irish Wake held at Finnegan's Pub in New Haven on Friday night from 5:00pm til close."

"What the hell?!" Jim groused, as he quickly folded the paper back up and reached for his cell phone.

He called the contact number on the inside of the paper. Someone answered on the 5th ring.

"Obits and op-eds," the voice said.

"Hello. This is Jim Reilly calling. This morning, you guys ran an obituary for me, but as you can hear, it was a bit pre-mature. I'm clearly not dead."

"Interesting. Well, we just run what people give us to run," the man responded.

"Who gave it to you? It had to be submitted online. You should be able to trace the payment or server," Jim insisted.

"Let me have a look. What was the name again?"

"Jim Reilly. James Reilly."

"Forty-five years old from Stratford?"

"Yes."

"It says here it was actually dropped off in person along with the payment."

"But who paid?"

"That it doesn't say. Paid in cash apparently."

"Cash?? Who pays in cash these days?" Jim asked.

"Apparently this person did."

"Well, you need to write a retraction."

"I'm not sure we do retractions."

"What do you mean you don't do retractions?"

"We've never had someone come back from the dead before."

"I was never dead. Someone is obviously playing some sort of sick joke."

"I suppose if you can get us proof you are alive, we might be able to get something in next week."

"Next *week*?? People will be upset. Some might even be hysterical. You need to take care of this straight away."

"Let me talk to my boss. This is a bit unusual. Not sure what we would call it. Obituary comes from the Latin word, obit, which means death."

"Call it a Vitauary then. From the Latin word for life! Just get this sorted!" Jim huffed as he hung up.

He immediately dialed another number.

"Aaron Harrington," the voice on the other end answered.

"It's Jim. What are you up to?"

"I'm at work," Aaron said, sounding puzzled.

"Can you break away?"

"I suppose so. Is everything ok?"

"No. But I'll explain when I see you. Let's meet at the Sitting Duck in 20 minutes," Jim said.

The bar was a local watering hole whose clientele hadn't changed much in the past 20 years. Dark, not necessarily dingy, but not immaculate either. Jim grabbed a table near the back of the bar and ordered a Guinness while he waited for Aaron. It was a bit early for a drink, but surely if there was an occasion that warranted it, it had to be your death. He skipped the customary greetings when Aaron arrived, opting instead to shove the paper in his face and point to the article in question. "Read this."

"Well, hello!" Aaron exclaimed. "Haven't spoken to you in weeks. Haven't seen you in months, but let's skip the pleasantries and shove a paper in my face."

"Just read it," Jim insisted.

Aaron glanced at it casually at first, before a bemused look overtook his face as he read on. "Is this some kind of joke?"

"You tell me," Jim answered.

"Whoever wrote this has you pegged pretty spot on," Aaron laughed.

"What do you mean?"

"Just mean that whoever wrote it must know you pretty well. So who did write it?"

"I have no idea. The person paid cash and dropped it off in person. And the paper is saying it could take a few days to get a retraction in."

"Well, I wouldn't worry too much about it. After all, you are alive. And I don't think most people our age tend to scour the obits on a daily basis. We're not 90."

"It only takes one," Jim insisted. "Then they tell someone, who tells someone else. With social media the way it is these days, the news could already be everywhere, and I don't want people wasting money flying clear across the country to attend my funeral."

"People don't fly across the country to attend a wake or funeral. They send flowers. But you might want to try and reach your brother just in case."

"Should we post something on Facebook?" Jim asked.

"Like what? I'm not dead?" Aaron laughed.

"Well, yeah."

"Look, I think you're looking at this all wrong," Aaron said. "You've got the opportunity to attend your own funeral. While you're alive no less. How cool is that?"

Jim appeared to be thinking about that. It was an intriguing concept. "What if no one showed up? That would be pretty embarrassing."

"I wouldn't rule that out as a possibility," Aaron said. "You have been kind of a salty recluse for the past few years. "Don't get me wrong," he quickly added when he saw Jim's face turn sour, "I understand why."

"I have not been a salty recluse," Jim responded defensively.

"You don't go anywhere. You don't do anything. You haven't written a word since she passed away.

"She was my wife. And the love of my life."

"I get that, but she was my sister and I loved her too. And I *know* she wouldn't have wanted us wallowing in misery at her leaving us. If you're honest with yourself, you know that too."

When Jim didn't respond, Aaron took that as a small victory.

"Tell you what," Aaron said, "I'll make some calls to see what I can find out. You should call your brother. And let's plan to go to this wake."

"I'm not going to the wake. That's creepy."

"It's the least you could do for the people that show up."

"I didn't invite them. I didn't tell anyone I was dead. I don't owe them anything."

Not taking "no" for an answer, Aaron said, "I'll pick you up Friday at 4:15 so we can get a table in the balcony. It's good to see you out and about."

Jim watched his brother-in-law leave while slowly sipping his Guinness. He touched the name "Sam" under his list of contacts and held the phone to his ear. After the 4th ring, Sam's voicemail picked up.

"You've reached Sam. Unfortunately, I can't get to the phone right now because I'm probably scaling Mt Everest, bungy jumping in the Everglades, whale watching in Cabo or some other crazy shit like that."

But instead of a BEEP that would allow Jim to leave a message, the voice message said the voice mail was "full" and "could not accept any messages."

He pressed the red button to end the call and continued to slowly drink his beer.

II THE STORY OF US

Most great love stories begin with "it was love at first sight." But what if it wasn't? Would it make it any less great? Or could it even be greater?

Rachelle Harrington came from a blue collar, middle class upbringing determined to leave that economic status behind. Her father was an electrician, beloved by everyone in their small Connecticut town, while her mother worked as a bank teller. Rachelle herself turned down an offer in high school to be a cheerleader, because it would have taken too much time away from her after school job working as a sandwich artist at Subway. Unfortunately, the 30+ hours a week she worked affected her grades. They were solid, but not Ivy League material, and the next tier schools did not have the same endowments that would enable a kid from a lower middle class family to afford the costs. So state school it was. She commuted the 30 minutes from home to save money, and worked in the dining hall for books and spending money. Her parents helped as much as they could and she graduated with minimal loans. But then it was on to law school at the University of Notre Dame, where the costs were significant--to the tune of nearly $70,000 per year.

Rachelle worked in the athletic department for home contests, wiping up sweat during stoppages in play at the basketball games, and mopping the floor during timeouts and halftime, completely oblivious to the catcalls and whistling from the boys in the student section that thought she was cute.

Three years later, she graduated in the middle of her law school class, but perspective employers were so impressed by her in person interviews, that she received three offers shortly after graduation. She settled on a job at the largest law firm in D.C. with her eyes set on an eventual career in politics, when fate intervened. Her father became ill, so she immediately moved back to Connecticut to help her mother care for him. She was offered a job as a public defender in the town she grew up in, with long hours and low pay--the exact opposite of what most people looked for in a job. But she was grateful to have one at all. Even with insurance, the cost of care for her father was high, so she had to take a second job cleaning public buildings in town on the night shift. One of the buildings she cleaned was the one where she worked during the day. Between her father and law school, her debt was more than two hundred and fifty thousand dollars and she wondered if she would ever be able to climb out from underneath it. And then one day, she didn't need to.

***

Jim Reilly had been raised with a silver spoon, but was more comfortable with a simple lifestyle. He was the son of a hedge fund manager and a doctor, who both made sure he never went without, but also never spoiled him. Yes, he had attended the same private school from 3rd grade until he graduated from high school, but that was because the public school in the town he lived in was so large, that they wanted to make certain he was able to participate in whatever school activities he desired, whether it be sports, student government or theatre. He chose sports, a three sport athlete who was good enough to star at his small school in all three, but likely would have been good enough to merely be on the team in two of them at the public school in town, only one of which, basketball, would he still have been a star.

Unlike many of his classmates, his parents never bought a car for him until his junior year of college, and even then it was a twice-used beater on its last legs. One day it simply wouldn't start no matter how many mechanics tried, so he sold it for parts and bought a bicycle. The thought never even crossed his mind to ask his parents for a replacement car even though they could have bought him a dealership instead.

The one problem that went with coming out of college without loans was that he didn't appreciate what he was supposed to be learning while he was there. Attending that 8:00am class would have taken on a whole new meaning if he had been the one paying for it. So he might have slept through more than his share of classes and sidestepped a few assignments. Those efforts translated into a couple of failed classes, not enough to flunk out, but enough that he needed a 5th year to graduate. His parents paid for that too, although they thought very seriously about not covering it. It was the last non-Christmas or birthday gift they ever gave him.

Jim eventually graduated with a slightly less than impressive GPA, but he wasn't without a set of accomplishments. He set a freshman record for most classes cut in a semester, year and college career while still obtaining his degree. He once nearly drank a case of beer in four hours, surpassing the previous record of 20 beers, set by a classmate who would go on to become a teacher and one day save a little boy from drowning. Jim followed a similar path of working with kids after graduation, minus the heroism, taking a job running the Park and Recreation Department in his hometown. It wasn't glamorous or high paying, but he didn't mind that, because he felt as though his interactions with children and adults on a daily basis, was making a difference in all of their lives. His job was really to make people feel better after a long day at school or work by giving them something fun to do. Something that made them feel a little better after they left than they had when they arrived. And he was good at it.

He was also a talented writer that spent most of his spare time writing. In the irony of ironies, many of the assignments he had "sidestepped" in college were novels he was supposed to have read for his American literature classes. Some time after graduation, he picked up one of the novels, a Pulitzer Prize winning book by an author who had died before its publication, and he didn't put it back down until he had finished it.   Then he picked up another.   And another.   And another. Eventually, he formed a small publishing company and tried his hand at writing his own novel. The book was well received, but hadn't yet found a very large audience when he decided to take matters into his own hands. Gathering up every last bit of savings and loose change he had--$5,273.22--he bought enough copies of his book to skyrocket it up the best seller lists to the point where it was visible to a whole new audience. It did the trick, as his book sales tripled in the weeks that followed. Three years, seven books and forty-five million sales later, he was a millionaire many times over, one hundred and fifty-two times to be exact.

And yet, he remained working the exact same job for the simple reason that he enjoyed it because it enabled him to interact with people, and people were the backbone of any story he wrote. His stories were all based on either an interesting person, or an interesting event, that he created a story around. They were all character driven and upbeat.   If you were looking for a sad ending, move on, because he believed life could be depressing enough without creating a story that was depressing. There was something special about the idea of creating stories that made people feel a little bit better after they had read it than they had before. Something special about creating flawed yet likable characters that were so heroic you wished you could be just like them. And his job enabled him to meet such people.

He usually wrote early in the morning or late at night in the peace and quiet of his office. It was easier than packing up, heading home, then unpacking and trying to motivate himself to write. One such night, the door to his office opened, and a girl from the nighttime cleaning crew stopped with a start.

"I'm so sorry," she said. "I didn't know anyone was still here."

"It's not a problem at all," Jim responded. "Do you need me to leave?"

"I can come back later if you like. I don't want to disturb you."

"You're doing me a favor actually. I haven't written a word in an hour."

"You're a writer?"

"Sometimes," he answered. Jim loved the anonymity being a writer afforded him. "Ok if I come back in a half hour or so?"

"That would be fine," she said.

And that was the extent of their first conversation. The next time he saw her, however, he noticed that her hands were perfectly manicured and her hair, which was pulled back into a tight ponytail high on top of her head, was long and silky smooth when she let it down temporarily to readjust it. He began to imagine what this girl's background was and decided to create a story around it. She was well spoken and well versed on political events, which made him think she was extremely bright, but life had thrown her a curveball or two. In his mind, she was a single mother, who had a child when she was young and was working multiple jobs in order to provide the best life for her child that she could. He envisioned one of the jobs involved working in an office, hence the nails and makeup. The second job was cleaning on the night shift because it didn't interfere with her other job. She was pretty enough, once you searched through the disguise, that she could have also worked as a bartender on the weekends.

It took him three conversations to learn her name--Rachelle--and seventeen conversations to find out he was underestimating the heroism of this young lady. She was a lawyer, a low earning one at that, who didn't have any kids and had never been married. Her father was ill and she had given up a very good job in D.C. to come home and help her mother care for him she explained. She now worked two jobs because she was heavily in debt.

Since his own family didn't need any money, Jim had always told himself if he ever came into big money himself, he would choose two families each Christmas to help with an extraordinary gift. The first time he did it, he chose a friend he had grown up with who was one of the hardest working people he knew, with very little financially to show for it. He had a wife, a mortgage, and would soon have two kids in college, if, he could afford to send them. Jim slipped a check into a Christmas card that he dropped off at their house, along with a bottle of wine. His friend opened the card, saw a check for one million dollars inside and promptly passed out. He hit his head so hard on the floor that he had to be rushed to the hospital. When he came to, Jim had to deal with an hour long argument about how they couldn't accept the check, before Jim finally convinced them the check wouldn't even dent a year's interest on his bank accounts. He felt like such a pompous ass for saying it even though it was true, that he decided from that moment on to donate money anonymously.

He usually did it by getting a check somehow for some reason from the person he was going to help. If it was someone he knew well, he'd ask if they wanted to go in on a Christmas gift for a mutual friend and have them reimburse him with a check. On the check was the bank's routing number and his or her checking account number. He'd then wire the amount directly into their account and they'd have no idea where it came from. When they asked the bank, they'd simply be told the person wished to remain anonymous.

"Question for you," he asked Rachelle late one night about a week before Christmas. "Don't feel as though you have to, but I'm helping collect for the United Way if you're interested. Any amount helps."

He felt terribly even asking her, knowing her financial situation, but it was the only way he could think of to get her bank account information. When she offered to give cash, he asked if she could write a check instead, so they could properly recognize everyone who donated. She showed up the very next night with a check for $25.

"I wish I could give more," she said.

"It's more than enough. Thank you."

Two days later, her twenty-five dollars had turned into one million and her financial worries were a thing of the past. Jim was the first person she suspected, but she quickly dismissed the thought because she didn't see how a city worker could possibly have that kind of money. She knew he wrote, but she had no idea how successful a writer he was. She didn't even know his last name. One afternoon, while perusing through some books at Barnes and Noble, a title caught her eye. _The Music Box_. A friend had told her about it. It was a story of a dying man whose one wish was to spend his remaining days with his estranged son. In the story, father and son spend their days listening to music from an old music box that has the ability to transport them back to the time his father first heard the songs. In the process the boy gets to not only see who his father really is, but also learns some valuable life lessons along the way. Rachelle flipped to the back cover and froze at the sight of the author's picture. "More than forty million books sold" the inside flap said. And she realized her initial instinct had been correct.

III WAKE ME UP BEFORE YOU GO GO

*"H*ave you found anything out?" Jim asked.

"Not really," Aaron responded over the phone.

"Well, did you at least put something on Facebook?"

"Something like what? Jim Reilly isn't dead?"

"That would probably work," Jim shrugged.

"Why don't you post something?" Aaron asked.

"Because I don't go on Facebook or any of those social media outlets."

"Because you're a curmudgeon."

"I'm not a curmudgeon. I just don't care to find out what's happening with someone I never liked 30 years ago."

"Any luck with the paper?"

"They said they'll be running something Monday. Which doesn't really help at all since the wake is Saturday."

"I've been thinking about that. You want to find out who did this correct?"

"Thank you, Captain Obvious."

"If we post something and cancel the wake, we'll probably never know. But here's my thought. We should go early and watch who shows up from the third tier of the bar. After a while, I'll go down and start interrogating people in a completely innocuous manner. Then, once people are good and sauced, you walk down the staircase and see who's surprised to see you. The one who isn't, is the guilty party."

"That's your great plan?" Jim asked skeptically.

"Well, my first thought was we ask the owner if we could bring a casket into the bar. We dress you in your Sunday finest and place you inside it with the lid open of course. You lie still until everyone has assembled and then you *pop* up without saying a word, with your eyes open wide!"

"You need help."

"If I'm honest, I'd be a little worried someone might have a heart attack on the spot if we went that route. Did you reach Sam?"

"No luck. My guess is he's out of the country as usual. Which is fine. At least he won't know about any of this."

"So you want me to pick you up at 4:30?" Aaron asked hopefully.

"Better make it 4:00," Jim responded. "If we don't want anyone to see us."

"Done."

***

Finnegan's was an Irish bar that had been converted from a church. Apparently, more people liked to drink than pray. It had raised ceilings and stained glass windows on its three levels, all of which looked down onto the oversized, rectangular shaped bar on the main floor. The third floor had been cordoned off for regular customers, with its own entrance on the side of the building. Aaron and Mike had arrived at 4:30 and took a seat on the third level so they could observe the action below them. At 4:45, the first person walked in towing a small suitcase by the handle. He was clearly an out of towner who had probably come straight from the train station to the bar. By 5:15 the entire first floor and most of the second were completely filled. By 5:45, it was starting to look like a mosh pit, but no one seemed to mind. The max occupancy of the place listed on the poster by the entrance was 500, but there looked to be at least 700 inside the first two levels of the bar by 6:00pm.

"There's a shitload of people in here," Aaron remarked.

"You seem surprised," Jim said.

"Well, you are a bit of a dickhead."

"That's really nice."

"I'm just sayin. You didn't used to be. But lately...."

"I know. I know," Jim responded, softening a little.

Seeing a tiny window, Aaron asked, "You ready for another drink?"

"Nah, I'm good."

"Jesus. In the old days, I'd hand you a drink, turn to the bar to grab mine, and by the time I turned back around, you'd already be done. Now, you're the slowest damn drinker I've ever seen. You want a binky to go with that beer?"

"Fine. I'll have another."

Aaron motioned to the waitress to bring another round. "Do you know all these people?"

Jim nodded as he looked over the rail. "Yeah. Most of them. Some of them got really old."

"I don't want to crap in your cornflakes, but so have you."

"That's a fair point."

"I'm going down," Aaron said.

"What are you going to say?"

"Just going to introduce myself around and see what I can find out."

He took the elevator down to the first floor and the doors opened to complete madness. At most Irish wakes, people came in for a drink or two, then buggered off as the next round of people showed. Only the close friends and family stayed around all night. But no one was showing any signs of leaving this wake anytime soon.

The first person Aaron saw when he stepped off the elevator was one of Jim's college roommates. He had been a groomsmen in Jim's wedding, and although Aaron hadn't seen him much since then, they had hit it off well that weekend.

"Aaron," Pete nodded as he pulled him in for a man hug.

"How are you, Pete? It's been a long time."

"I couldn't believe it when I heard the news. I know Jim took it hard when Rachelle passed and had become a bit of a recluse, but I didn't know he was sick himself. I spoke to him about a month ago and he didn't say a word."

"That's because he wasn't," Aaron answered.

"Then how did he die?"

"Hungarian Bird Flu."

"Whaaat?"

Aaron nodded. "Woke up one morning with a cold. It soon moved into his chest. Two days later, he was gone."

"Are you joking?"

"Nope. Apparently, somebody brought it into the tri-state area through JFK Airport."

"Jesus. I've been battling a cold for the last few days."

"Better be careful," Aaron warned.

The next person he ran into was wearing an LL Bean jacket over a pink button down Oxford, a pair of wide cords and penny loafers *with* the pennies in them. He guessed the guy's name was Biff, Skip or Chip before he spoke.

"I was Jim's brother-in-law," Aaron said by way of introduction.

"I'm Chad," the man said. That was Aaron's next guess. "I went to high school with Jim. In fact, I actually live in Connecticut, down in Greenwich, but I don't get up this way that often. I hadn't spoken to Jim in quite a few years. What happened to him if you don't mind my asking?"

"He was killed in a hot air balloon accident. The flame burned a hole in the liner of the balloon at 10,000 feet and it came crashing down. Pbfffft," Aaron answered, making a raspberry sound for emphasis.

"Oh my god," Chad responded with a look of horror on his face.

Aaron continued to work his way through the crowd, shaking the hands of familiar faces as he went.

"Aaron. How are you?" a man asked. He was youngish, with dark hair and a scruffy beard. The suit he was wearing didn't fit him quite right, and looked as though it hadn't been worn in years.

"I'm hanging in there, Tommy. Thanks for coming."

"Was Jim sick?" the man asked.

"Nope."

"I saw him Monday at work. Then Tuesday morning I heard he was gone."

"Here's the thing. Not many people know this but Jim spent his evenings as an underground MMA fighter. Monday night, he got kicked in the head and was knocked unconscious. He slipped into a coma and died a few hours later."

"Jim? Jim Reilly?" the man repeated incredulously. "He didn't strike me as much of a fighter.

"Well, he wasn't a very good one. Which is probably why he got killed."

"Are you Aaron?" another man asked.
"Yes."
"I was Jim's editor."
"Of course. Cindi right?"
"Yes.   Someone told me he died in a bungy jumping accident. Is that true?"
"No. He was learning to fly a Cesna and ran it into the side of Mt. Southington. I'm surprised you didn't see it on the news."

Aaron turned around, very pleased with himself. He was enjoying this and figured they deserved every ridiculous answer he gave them. They had broken the cardinal rule of a wake. Never ask how a person died. If you were supposed to know, you would already know. He took a sip of his beer, and found himself confronted by a woman he didn't know, who was about his age.

"I'm Heather Palmer. I went to high school with Jim.   And you sir, are completely full of shit," she said.

"I beg your pardon?" Aaron smirked.

"Jim did not die of the Hungarian Bird Flu, or in a hot air balloon, or in an MMA fight, or by flying his plane into Mt. Southington."

"Are you stalking me? And how do you know?"

"Because I just do."

Aaron eyed her suspiciously. "But how?"

"Because those are ridiculous answers. There have been no reported cases of Hungarian Bird Flu in the states for at least ten years. Hot air balloons are fire resistant. Jim hated the movie *Fight Club*. And he was also afraid of flying."

"Well, when you ask an obnoxious question, you get an obnoxious answer," Aaron smiled. "Besides, I thought they all sounded better than he went to sleep one night and never woke up."

"You could at least send him out as a ladies man. Tell people he had a heart attack after being
found in bed with four Hawaiian Tropic models."

"Anyone who knew him would never believe that."

"That's a good point. I practically threw myself at him in high school and never got more than a high five," she laughed.

"Now *that* is very believable."

"I hadn't seen him in years. I thought about reaching out to see how he was doing after he lost his wife, but I didn't want to bother him. His wife was your sister, right?"

"Yes."

"She was beautiful."

"Yes she was. And smart. The two of them made a really nice couple. At least now they're together again."

Aaron's phone buzzed. A text message from Jim read, *"How long is this going to go on?"*

Aaron responded with, *"I think now would be a good time to make your entrance. I have a potential suspect. Wait for my cue and then walk down the stairs. It will be more dramatic than taking the elevator."*

"Can you excuse me for a second?" he said to Heather.

"Of course."

Aaron climbed on top of the bar and raised his hands in the air to quiet the crowd. "I want to thank everyone for coming tonight," he began. "For those of you who don't know me, and I think that's most of you, I'm Aaron Harrington. I was Jim Reilly's brother-in-law. To be completely honest, as I'm sure someone in this rooms knows, I still am."

There was a noticeable buzz in the room as people struggled to understand what he was talking about.

"Jimbo..." he continued, looking up the winding staircase toward the upper levels.

After the uncomfortable few seconds that followed, Jim appeared out of the darkness and began descending the stairs. A palatable feeling of anger, confusion and shock overtook the room. Two women feinted at the very sight of him.

"Now might be as good a time as any for the person who reported Jim as dead to come forward," Aaron offered.

No one uttered a word. Heather Palmer simply smiled.

IV PETE HOWARD

Pete Howard arrived at the University of Notre Dame as so many others had before him, talented in the small pond he grew up in, but now surrounded by equally, if not more talented people. Although sharing an experience with people from similar backgrounds was comforting initially, it was also a bit disheartening as you tried to stand out from the crowd.

Pete's issue was that any success he had growing up, whether it be in athletics, academically or otherwise, had been done quietly. He was the person you needed to meet two or three times before you realized he had an amazingly understated sense of humor and razor sharp intellect regarding nearly any topic. His problem was that he was quiet to a fault, not necessarily because he was shy, although there might have been some of that too, but more so because he thought the best way to learn was to listen.

Jim Reilly and Pete Howard first met in the lobby of their dormitory in college while

Pete was on the pay phone. This was a time when there actually *were* pay phones, cell phones were scarce, as large as a toaster, and a call cost the same as a second mortgage.

"Problems with the girlfriend?" were the first words Jim ever spoke to him.

"Yeah, she's off the rails. Can't handle the distance between us so she doesn't want to talk for a while."

"Huh?"

"I don't get it either. She's upset because I went away to school, but doesn't want to talk to me and doesn't want me to go home for the weekend."

Jim nodded as if he understood completely.

"What?" Pete asked.

"Well, we don't know each other so I probably should mind my own business," Jim responded.

"I'm Pete," he said, extending his hand. "Now we know each other. I'm open to all suggestions."

"Jim Reilly," Jim answered. "Here's the thing, seeing as I'm a senior now, I see this every year. Your girlfriend is pissed you left, so she's going to look for someone else to occupy her time. Sounds harsh I know. But she's a girl and completely incapable of being alone, so that's how it works. So you have two choices. 1) Transfer to a college back home.   Which I don't recommend. Exactly one of my friends from high school are still with their high school girl friends. And no one I know that's older actually married them."

"What's the second choice?" Pete asked.

"Shift her focus and get her wanting you. Women like the chase as much as men. They just don't admit it."

"And how do I do that?"

"That's as easy as a Sunday morning, my friend," Jim said. "First of all, you don't call her."

"Ever?"

"That's kind of the idea behind not calling someone."

"But then how do I get her back?"

"After a few days, she'll call you. And when she does, act nice and happy to hear from her, but tell her you're on your way out to play basketball with your roommates. Ask her if you can call her later. And then don't call."

"I'm not following you."

"She'll call you the next day wanting to fight, but you apologize and tell her you guys played for like four hours. When you came back, you sat down on the couch for five minutes because you were exhausted.

Next thing you know, it was morning. Then tell her you have to run to work on a class project, but you'll call her later."

"Let me guess. Then I don't call her," Pete said dryly.

"No, this time you call her. But you tell her you only have a minute before you're going to mass."

"I haven't gone to mass in ages."

"She doesn't need to know that. Every time you speak to her, you act extremely friendly. Even tell her you were just thinking about her. But you're always headed out the door. Not to parties, but to things she can't possibly get pissed about. She'll be really confused. You're being nice, but you're busy all the time and seem perfectly happy without her. After a couple of weeks, she'll be begging to get back together."

***

"So did the plan work?" Aaron asked as Jim relayed the story while bellied up to the bar at Finnegan's. The wake continued on all around them, with people stopping to shake his hand and pat him on the back as they walked past.

"Hell yes, it worked," Jim answered while Pete nodded in agreement.

"You got back together?"

"For a couple of weeks," Pete said.

"You are like a relationship Zen master!" Aaron exclaimed.

"What can I say? I know women," Jim responded.

"You don't know them that well," Heather Palmer interjected.

"What makes you say that?" Aaron asked. "And you just love to eavesdrop, don't you?"

"I practically threw myself at Jim in high school."

"You most certainly did not," Jim answered.

"I sat next to you in four classes. I went to all of your basketball games. When that didn't work, I even became a cheerleader. And I *hate* cheerleaders. But you didn't give me the time of day."

"I love cheerleaders," Pete said quietly.

"I was nice," Jim protested.

"I didn't say you weren't nice. I said you were clueless. Never asked me out once."

"I never asked anyone out in high school."

"And why is that?"

"I guess I was waiting for the lightning bolt to hit and wasn't going to settle until it did. Not that being with you would have been settling. I just am a believer in the principle of the moment. The moment when you realize the person you like, feels the same way about you."

"And were you struck by lightning when you first met Rachelle?" Heather asked.

"To be honest, no. She came in to clean my office and we barely spoke. But each time she came in, we spoke a little more. I made sure I stayed until she came, and I think she made sure to come to my office at the exact same time, although she would have denied that. As I got to know her better, I began to realize what an incredible person she was. Gave up a good job to come home and help care for her sick father. Worked two jobs to pay the bills. I liked her very much. Then one night, she let her hair down to fix her scrunchie, and I was done. How on earth I hadn't recognized how beautiful she was before that moment is beyond me. Maybe she intended it to be that way. Maybe she wanted me to like her as a person first. Whatever it was, my life was never the same again. And without her, I'm worried it never will be."

They were all silent after he finished speaking. What was there to say after that?

"Way to take the air out of the conversation, Jimbo," Pete said stoically and everyone laughed.

"I can't believe you came all the way from California for this," Jim responded. "I told Aaron we should put something on social media letting everyone know it was someone's idea of a joke, but he said, and I quote *'People don't fly across the country for a funeral. They send flowers.'*"

Aaron winced. He had said that.

"No worries. I would have flown across country just to hang out with you. It's been too long."

"Yes, it has," Jim agreed. Turning to Aaron and Heather he said, "Pete won't toot his own horn, but he runs one of the most successful hedge funds in the country. He was on Forbes Top 30 Wealthiest people in California under 30 when he was 27, and he was 152nd on Forbes 400 wealthiest people in the United States last year. He's so rich, if he was single, women would probably overlook how incredibly awkward he is around them."

"Well, thank you for that. I think," Pete laughed. "Talk about a backhanded compliment."

Chad Whitbeck approached and invited himself into the conversation. "Glad you're still alive, Jim."

"Thanks, Chad. How are you? It's been a while."

"I'm terrific. What investment company do you work for?" he asked Pete.

"Santa Clara Investment Group," Pete answered.

"Oh that's a nice little group," Chad responded. "I'm with APM down in Greenwich."

"APM?" Aaron asked.

"Advanced Planning Management. We're #1 on Forbes most recent list."

"Is that so?"

"Yup," Chad nodded, completely oblivious to how he was being perceived. "Anyone need a drink?"

"Definitely need a drink," Aaron said. "Two Stella's, what are you drinking, Heather?"

"The house Chardonnay."

"I'll get you a nice wine," Chad assured her. "Santa Clara?"

"I'll try the local beer. Two Roads," Pete answered.

Aaron barely waited for Chad to be out of earshot before he said, "What a giant ballbag."

Heather laughed. "What on earth is a ballbag? Or do I not want to know?"

"What's the first word that comes to mind when you meet that guy?" Aaron asked.

"Rich," Pete said. "Actually two words. Filthy rich. He's right about his company. And if that's Chad Whitbeck, he's the 25th richest person in the country."

"It is Chad Whitbeck," Jim nodded. "Heather and I went to high school with him."

"Ok, other than filthy rich, what word comes to mind when you speak to that guy?" Aaron pressed.

"Annoying," Heather answered.

"*That* is what a ballbag is. The fact that he looks like Lurch from the Adams Family makes him a *giant* ballbag."

"So here we are, having dragged all these people here for a phony wake, and we're no closer to finding out who's responsible than we were when we started," Jim lamented.

"Maybe not. But no one seems to mind," Aaron answered.

"What do we do now?"

"There's only one thing *to* do. It's time for some shots."

"Chad just went to get us drinks. What if he can't find us?"

"We should be so lucky," Aaron said. "Let's go to the second floor."

V THE HIGH SCHOOL GIRL "FRIEND"

As the daughter of two teachers, Heather Palmer's career path was pre-determined for her. Unlike some people who sort of "fell" into teaching after a few other choices didn't pan out, for Heather, teaching was the only thing she ever wanted to do. She decided to attend state school, in part because it was the cheapest option, but also because it was the most direct way to achieve her certification. Once she made that choice, the remainder of her career path chose itself.

Her friends came and went, but knowing it was easier to get certified in the state where she attended college, Heather never did leave Connecticut, save for one or two stray vacations that she took. She was happy enough doing something she loved and being around her family, even if her circle of friends was a bit eclectic and had an age range that spanned nearly five decades.

The only thing she was missing was romance, but elementary schools were not exactly brimming with the possibilities of young, available, heterosexual men. She tried a few dating sites, but found her dates to be sketchy, needy or desperate. Some of them were all three. The amazing thing was that Heather was smart, funny and beautiful. Not just beautiful in a traditional way. Really strikingly stunning. With silky smooth shoulder length brown hair, surrounding deep, soulful brown eyes that were as wide as saucers. She was tall and thin, and knew how to walk like a woman, with key parts all moving in the appropriate direction every time she took a step. And yet, she remained alone. Her friends told her it was her curse. She was too beautiful and men either assumed she was taken or were too intimidated to find out. The thing was, all she really wanted was a guy who was nice to her and made her laugh.

As the years passed, she lamented the wasted time in high school where she pined for a guy who had sentenced her to life in the friend zone with no opportunity for parole. Eventually, he too got married, but just when Heather was about to give up on romance altogether, her crush's wife passed away. Heather waited an appropriate amount of time before trying to get him out for dinner, but before she succeeded, he died as well. And then, just as suddenly, he came back to life.

***

"How is it you're still single?" Jim asked, after throwing back a shot of vodka and slamming it onto the bar. He had loosened up considerably since walking in the door of his wake.

"What do you mean?"

"You're beautiful," he said matter-of-factly.

"Then how come you never asked me out?"

"Because we were friends."

"We didn't have to be."

"What's wrong with being friends?" Jim asked.

"My god. Please just slap me across the face next time. Anything but that."

"You were like a sister to me."

"You know, some people have actually found me attractive."

"I'm sure they have."

"Just not you," Heather responded wryly.

"I've always thought you were attractive. You're a hottie," he smiled.

"Now you're reaching," she laughed. "It's fine, I'll die a lonely old spinster, with a really nice ass and perfect tits."

Alcohol was fueling the conversation now.

"Who's got a really nice ass and perfect tits?" Tommy asked as he walked up.

"She does," Pete said, pointing at Heather.

"I can see that," Tommy agreed.

Everyone laughed, before Jim suddenly turned to Aaron and said, "Are you kidding me?"

"What?" he responded with the faintest hint of a smirk.

"There's a lady here, and you decided to just pass gas like you're in your bathroom at home."

The smirk soon turned into a full-fledged grin. "It's not healthy to hold it in."

"You better hold it in, or I'm going to grab one of those limes you've been dropping into your beers all night and cork you with it."

"That's awful," Tommy said.

"My eyes are watering," Jim said.

"Now you're exaggerating," Aaron said, defending himself.

"I wish I could cut my nose off with a pair of scissors," Pete deadpanned as Heather burst out laughing.

"We're going to leave now, and go to the other side of the room," Jim said. "I want you to sit here and do some serious soul searching about what you just did. After you've reflected for an appropriate amount of time, *maybe* you can rejoin us. You smelly bastard."

And they all walked away, leaving Aaron surrounded by a fog of his own making, a little more pleased with himself than perhaps he should have been.

VI THE CO-WORKER

Tommy Waters was raised by a single mother in one of the most socially and racially diverse towns in the state of Connecticut. The home of Sikorsky Aircraft, Stratford was a two high school town in a town that should have probably had one. Tommy's classmates included the sons and daughters of Sikorsky executives, small business owners as well as single parent households like his, where the parent had to work three different hourly jobs just to live paycheck to paycheck.

Tommy was extremely popular in school as a soccer star who also kicked field goals and extra points for the football team. Nicknamed the "Lil Kickin Man" by his teammates, anyone who had a problem with him would need to go through 40 to 50 people just to get to him.

He often had to go without--without new sneakers, a jacket, and even an occasional meal, but he believed going without is what helped him appreciate when things did go his way.   He loved his mother for her dedication to providing the best life for him she could and he loved the town he grew up in, which is the main reason he never left. He worked in the Park and Rec Department during his summer break, cutting the grass at the town fields and helping run the youth and adult recreation programs during the evenings.

After graduating from high school, he soon realized that college wasn't in the cards for him.   It was too expensive, even at the state schools, and the job market after graduation made it difficult to justify taking on that much debt.   As a result, he accepted a full time position at the Park and Rec Department working under Jim Reilly and went from being a paid intern to a co-worker overnight.   Soon after, their relationship became one of friendship.   Jim stood next to Tommy as his best man when he got married.   He and his wife waited for him in the waiting room on the days Tommy's children were born.   They celebrated holidays together.   And they mourned together.

Tommy was inconsolable by himself in the basement bathroom of the funeral home the day of Rachelle Reilly's funeral.   She had been like a second mother to him after his own had passed, even though she was only five years older than he was, and he only managed to pull himself together because he knew Jim needed the support. The truth of the matter was that no amount of support would help Jim. He withdrew from life following that day, going through the motions at his job, not writing a word, and rarely leaving the house. There were no more shared holidays. No more birthday celebrations. Sure, they spoke superficially at work, but it wasn't the same. Yet, Tommy never pressed him.

"You want to go get a beer?" he suggested one Tuesday night after the adult volleyball leagues had ended.

"Appreciate it, but I'm going to head home. I'm beat. Next time though," Jim answered.

Tommy figured Jim would come out of it in his own way in his own time and headed home. The following morning, while he made breakfast for his wife and two teenage children, a boy and a girl, his cell phone rang. It was a number he didn't recognize from a neighboring town. Normally, he wouldn't have answered. If it was important, they'd leave a message. But something inside him told him this call was different.

"Hello?" Tommy answered cautiously.

"Tommy. It's Tone."

"What's going on, Tone?" Tommy glanc-ed at the clock. It read 7:45am which was kind of an odd time for him to be calling.

"Listen. I'm in jail down in Bridgeport. I can't really explain why right now, but I will when I can. I need 50 grand in bail money to get me out and I'm seriously worried if I don't get out, I won't make it through the next 24 hours."

"50 grand? Jesus, man. I don't have that kind of money. There isn't anyone else you know that can help?"

Tommy knew Tone's family was scattered. His father had been in and out of prison. His mother was prone to running off with an assorted array of men and certainly wouldn't have it. Tommy heard Tone fell in with one of the street gangs and was dealing, but had left it alone. Some things he figured he was better off not knowing.

"There's no one, man. And I would never ask,

but I've got some bad people after me."

"Then aren't you safer in jail?"

"I'm a sitting duck in jail."

The truth of the matter was that Tommy did have 50 grand, $52,517.44 to be exact, which he and his wife had saved to give their kids a chance to experience something he never had a chance to--college. His first instinct was to call his wife. He could never make a decision like this without her input. But she was a teacher and likely in class. The call went straight to voice mail.

In the end, he always had a soft spot for Tone. He had always wanted a better life, but had never gotten a break. And Tommy decided he could never live with himself if something happened to him and he didn't try to help. Besides, it was only a loan. He'd get it back once Tone's court case was settled.

At 9:00am on the dot, Tommy Waters walked into People's Bank and withdrew nearly all of their life savings. Thirty minutes later, he was walking briskly towards the jail when he heard footsteps behind him. It was an area of town where footsteps were nearly always a cause for concern even with the police station less than two blocks away. He turned and was relieved when he saw a uniformed officer behind him. Moments later, the officer was next him, his gun drawn. Tommy instinctively raised his arms over his head.

"What did I do?!" Tommy asked.

"Give me your wallet," the officer responded curtly.

"Excuse me? You serious?"

"Now!" the man shouted.

"Can I just give you the cash?"

The man ripped the wallet out of his hand. "What's in the backpack?"

"My lunch."

The fake officer took it off Tommy's shoulder and unzipped the back pouch. "Holy shit," he exclaimed before running down the nearest alley to a running automobile. At least the criminal drove an American car Tommy thought as he watched Tone's bail money, not to mention his kid's college education drive away in a Ford Fiesta. He filed a report at the police station and pleaded with the desk officer to release Tone, but the plea fell on deaf ears, as he knew it would. He was also late for work, but Jim wasn't in yet either to give him a hard time about it. He did find it strange when Jim still wasn't there and hadn't called two hours later. Just after noon, Tommy's phone rang. It was a Bridgeport Hospital extension.

"Mr. Waters?"

"Yes."

"You're listed as a contact for a Tone Jefferson."

"Contact for what?"

"He was pretty severely beaten in jail and has been admitted to Bridgeport Hospital."

"Is he ok??"

"He will be, but he's in tough shape right now."

"I'm on my way," Tommy said as he raced out of his office.

He thought about calling Jim, but he wasn't yet ready for a lecture. He entered Tone's hospital room after being checked by the armed guard outside it.

"Lil Kickin Man," Tone said quietly with a smile.

"I'm so sorry, man. I was on my way to pay your bail when I got robbed at gunpoint."

"You were?" he brightened.

"Don't look so happy about it. I could have gotten killed."

"Not happy you got robbed. Happy you were coming to help me. I knew you were the only one who would."

"Of course I would. I'm sorry I didn't get you out in time."

"It means a lot that you even tried. And I'll pay you back every dime."

Tommy knew he never would be able to, but knowing that he would if he could, would have to be good enough for now. He went back to his office and tried to figure out how to break the news of the day to his wife. He came to the conclusion that he was going to need to just rip off the Band-Aid and tell her. He snapped open the newspaper on his desk at about 4:00pm. He usually began his day by reading it, but this was no ordinary day. On Page 6, he found out why Jim Reilly wasn't at work that day, and never would be again. Tears began to stream down his face.

VII THE BROTHER-IN-LAW

"I can't believe you didn't tell me you were still alive," Tommy said at the bar, shaking his head.

"That's because *this* idiot told me not to say anything," Jim answered, pointing at Aaron.

"That was a definite lapse in judgment on your part," Pete interjected softly. "Even Aaron knows he's full of shit."

"You do make a good point. I definitely should have known better. The first time I ever met this guy was just after Rachelle and I got engaged. I went over to their parent's house for a celebratory family dinner. Aaron was living at home while going to college. But that afternoon, he tells his parents he has a project to work on over at the university library. His mother tells him to be back by 5:45 and he leaves. 5:45 comes and goes and no sign of Aaron. Then at 6 o'clock, he calls and says that his car won't start and he's just waiting for a friend to come jump it. Well, I had jumper cables in my car, so I tell his mother that I'll head over there. I try calling him on the way 5 or 6 times but he isn't answering. I get to the parking lot and see his car, but no sign of him. So I decide to go inside to look for him. The first floor is empty. So is the second floor. In fairness, it was almost 6:30 on a Friday night, so no real surprise there. I'm getting ready to leave when I hear some noise coming from the floor above. I go up the stairs and I'll be damned if it didn't look like a Jimmy Buffet concert when I stepped out of the stairwell. It was *packed*. The entire floor. Red solo cups everywhere. People were trying to be quiet, but they weren't very good at it. And every few minutes I would see a group of people disappear down one of the book stacks in the back. So I followed them, and what do I find? Idiot Aaron pouring cups of Genny Cream Ale out of a keg. Girls were flashing him to get a cup. Guys had to streak across the aisles and back to get one."

"They were throwing a library kegger?" Heather laughed. "That is incredible."

"I'll admit I was somewhat impressed. But it gets worse. The librarian gets pissed at the noise, security shows up, and everybody scatters. But Idiot Aaron grabs the keg and starts running down the stairs with it."

"Why on earth wouldn't you just leave it?" Tommy asked.

"Because kegs are traceable on account of the deposit. They would have found out I was the one responsible," Aaron answered.

"I give him credit for thinking of that. But it didn't make it any easier running down the stairs. At one point we dropped it and it smashed a hole into the stairwell wall. But we just pulled it back out and kept running," Jim said.

"How'd you guys get it *in* there to begin with?" Pete asked.

"We sent someone in through the front, and they went down the back stairwell and let us in through the back door. Believe me, it was twice as hard getting a full keg *up* the stairs," Aaron explained.

"We finally got to my truck and threw the keg in the back. He was obviously in no condition to drive so we left his car there and went back to his parent's house. Of course his mom was steaming at this point, but she didn't want to let on to that fact in front of her future son-in-law. So we're about halfway through dinner and it's pretty quiet. Just casual conversation. Then I notice Aaron weaving a back and forth in place and his eyes starting to close. Sure enough, about five seconds later, he goes face first into a pile of mashed potatoes. Splatters them all over his father. His mother starts screaming because she thinks he just had a heart attack. His father is ready to knock him out because he has mashed potato remnants all over his new shirt. Rachelle is sitting there in shock, embarrassed as hell. And I'm laughing hysterically because I know that he's just wasted and passed out."

Everyone was roaring with laughter now, including a few people who stopped their conversations to listen in on the story. Even Aaron was enjoying the laugh at his own expense because he hadn't seen Jim laugh that hard in a long time.

At that very moment, the double doors of the bar were thrown open and a man entered. He was wearing a backpack, cargo shorts, a t-shirt that had "Surf Santorini" written across the front, and a wide-brimmed sun hat. He was tan and smiling, with a grin that ran from ear to ear.

"Been crocodile hunting, have we?" Pete asked.

The man pointed directly at Jim. "You're supposed to be dead."

"I'm not," Jim answered.

The man shrugged as if he had told them they were out of Corona and simply said, "Well, then I guess you owe me a beer." Sam Reilly put his arm around his younger brother and shook him playfully as he sauntered up to the bar.

VIII SAM I AM

Growing up, Sam Reilly was popular for the simple reason that he was interesting. He wasn't a star athlete or a great student, but he called himself a professor of human behavior. Sam had the innate ability to say the perfect thing at exactly the right time, while also knowing when to be silent and listen.

He lived his life by the motto that he would try anything once. If he liked it, twice. But never more than that. In college, Sam once leaped off the roof of a house into a waiting snow bank wearing nothing but a smile and jumped into a pool while fully clothed. He was a member of *both* the Young Republicans and Liberal Student Society because he enjoyed hearing opposing views and trying to find middle ground. The athletes liked him because they knew he wouldn't have cared if they didn't. The theatre crowd took him in as one of their own because he was technologically savvy enough to help them put on their shows. He ran for Student Body President and won, on a platform that consisted of messages written on loose leaf notebook paper, tacked onto trees around campus, written in crayon. He had more friends than acquaintances and was the person everyone missed when he wasn't around. At graduation, he became the first person in school history to give the valedictorian speech with a 2.67 GPA. The actual valedictorian was the person who pushed for it.

While most of his friends would go on to careers as doctors, lawyers, accountants, and business men and women, Sam decided to build houses for Habitat for Humanity in Guatemala. When he lacked money, he took any job he could find. When his parents passed, they left Sam and Jim enough money that it was no longer an issue and he went where the winds blew him. He worked as a host for wine tastings at a vineyard in California. He worked on a fishing boat off the coast of Maine. He was a production manager for a Hollywood film set. He volunteered for the Red Cross whenever a natural disaster took place, sweeping into places ravaged by tornados, hurricanes, earthquakes, floods and forest fires. It was safe to say moss never grew beneath his feet because he never stayed in any one place long enough for that to happen.

His relationship with his brother was a complicated one. They enjoyed each other's company on those rare occasions they were actually together, but the way they looked at life was as different as night and day. Jim was a homebody who never left the town he grew up in except to go to college. He was loyal to the core, staying with the same woman, driving the same car, keeping in touch with the same friends his entire adult life.

Sam Reilly admired those traits in his brother, but had far bigger goals in mind for his life. He wanted to meet as many people as he could, make as many friends as could from all different walks and economic stratospheres as he could. He wanted to help people and he did. More than he could probably ever recount. But his transient lifestyle, left some of his friends, along with his brother, feeling left behind. As if complete strangers were more important to Sam than they were. And yet whenever he returned, they quickly forgave him. He had an enormous heart, and was so much fun to be around, they reveled in every minute of it, until he left again, at which point, a gigantic hole had been sucked out of their lives all over again.

***

"You look pretty good for a dead guy," Sam said.

"I'm really sorry about dragging you all the way here for this. I called you, but it went straight to voice mail and wouldn't let me leave a message," Jim answered.

"It's fine. My voice mail was full from people calling about you. So I called Aaron and he told me the truth."

"And you came anyway?"

"Of course. What kind of person would I be if I didn't attend my own brother's wake? Besides, it's been too long."

"Where have you been hiding these days? Swimming with the dolphins in St. Thomas? Crocodile hunting in the Australian Outback?"

"Santorini."

"Santa what?"

"Santorini. A beautiful Greek island full of beautiful Greeks. As well as assorted other beautiful people from around the world."

"Sounds exotic," Aaron said.

"It's amazing. Might be my favorite place ever. Built atop of a volcano in the southernmost part of the Aegean Sea. White washed buildings with roofs so blue they match the country's flag perfectly. The island has some of the most incredible views you've ever even heard about. Built into the hillside high up on the bluff, you step outside and feel as though the sea is part of your backyard. And the beaches? Red, white and black lava pebbles adorn them."

"What do you do there? Anything?"

"I'm tending bar at the business end of an infinity pool in a resort on top of the mountain. If you travel by boat, the only way to access the resort it is to either walk up hundreds of steps, ride a donkey, or take a cable car."

"Out of those choices, I'll go with C, Cable Car, final answer," Pete interjected.

"You should come visit. Heck, you should move there with me," Sam said to Jim.

"Why?" Jim laughed. "You'll be someplace new in a couple of months."

"Normally I would agree with you, but not this time," Sam corrected.

"Has to be a woman involved," Jim said. "You knock someone up?"

"No, I didn't knock someone up," Sam laughed.

"You say that like it is out of the realm of possibility," Jim chuckled.   "You get married?"

"Neither," Sam said. "But there is someone. We're in the early stages, but we have grown close. She's the daughter of a jewelry maker on the island. Beautiful. Smart. Gentle. Sweet."

"How old?"

"28."

"28?! She's half your age."

"I don't know who taught you math, but you should ask for a refund. I'm only 47."

"Still. Pretty young."

"Age is a number. Some people die in their 30's while some live to be 100. We have no way of knowing when our number will be called, so there's no sense worrying about it."

One of the bartenders approached, "Guys, you're welcome to stay and drink, but the open bar is closing up shortly."

"Open bar?" Jim said, spinning around. "Who paid for it?"

"That I don't know," the bartender said. "I just know it's been taken care of."

"We need to know who is responsible for all this. Can't you look at the receipt?" Jim persisted.

"It was paid for during the day to the person who handles our large groups. I could find out for you, but it wouldn't be until tomorrow."

"Aaron. You hear that? Tomorrow, we can find our man....or woman," Jim added with a look towards Heather.

"Don't look at me," she said. "I like you and all, but you're crazy if you think I picked up the tab for this party."

"Tomorrow, we worry about who did this," Aaron said with a grand sweeping gesture. "Tonight, we have a decision to make."

"Which is?" Jim asked.

"Do we stay here and continue to drink? Call it a night and go home? Or go someplace else?"

"Such as?"

"The casino," Sam said with a wink. "Blackjack. Roulette. Sports gambling. Food. Drinks. Dancing."

"I don't have any money to burn I'm afraid," Tommy said. "I'm only here because of the free booze."

"Don't worry about the money. I'll spot you. Anything you win, you keep. Anything you lose, you don't have to pay it back."

"When you put it like that, how can I refuse?" Tommy answered.

"You can't."

"That is a pretty good offer," Pete said. "Can I get the same one?"

"Hell no.   You're on Forbes list of wealthiest Americans.   You should spot everyone."

"Damn Forbes," Pete groused.   "Blowing up my spot."

"I'm in," Aaron said.

"Me too," Heather said.

All eyes were now on Jim.   "I don't know," he said at last.

"I'm not taking no for an answer," Sam said.   "I came all the way from Greece for your Fake Wake."

"Yes, I know.   Your beautiful Greek island with beautiful Greeks," Jim answered. "Fine. I'll go. It's not every day I get to hang out with my brother and my friends."

"Did I hear you guys say you were heading to the casino?" Chad asked, interjecting himself into the conversation. "I love the casino."

"Umm, yeah," Aaron said, "But I don't have any room in my car."

"No problem. I can fit someone with me. Only one though. You know, sports car. I'll meet you around front in five minutes."

"Don't even think about pawning me off on that Ball Pump, of whatever it is you called him," Heather said once they were outside.

"Ball*bag*," Aaron corrected. "And don't worry about it. Get in."

"Are we really going to all ride in one car and make Chad drive up there by himself?" Jim asked.

"Yup. The Denali waits for no ballbag," Aaron answered, as he shifted his SUV into gear and sped away from the curb.

IX BLACKJACK SAM

*T*he Denali pulled up to the valet area just outside the casino entrance and a man wearing a thick fur coat and cowboy hat opened the car doors for them. It wasn't that cold out, but Aaron supposed if you were outside for an eight hour shift, it might eventually wear on you. He did, however, find the choice of hat with that particular coat to be somewhat suspect. He decided to slip the guy a folded over Andy Jackson anyway along with the keys.

"Thank you, sir. I will keep it up top for a quick getaway," the man said.

"Well, I'm hoping it won't be *that* quick, but if we take the Indians for too much money and you see us running out the door, you'll know."

"I've have the keys ready," the man laughed.

"All right," Sam said, huddling the crew together just inside. "Blackjack first. We need to find an empty table so all six of us can play together. It won't be easy on a Friday night, so our choices will be limited to tables that are empty for a reason-- meaning they've been cleaning everyone's clocks all night. Or we can hit the high roller pit. Minimum bets usually start at $100 a hand in there."

"That means I could play about three hands," Heather laughed.

"I could play zero hands at those numbers," Tommy added.

"Don't worry about it. Pete, Jim, Aaron and I will bankroll you."

"Ummm," Aaron stuttered.

"Ok, ok. Pete, Jim and I will bankroll you. It works better if we have the whole table. That way no outsider is going to bitch about you staying on a 15. Plus, it helps throw them off if you have two or three clueless people playing. No offense."

"Thanks a lot," Aaron feigned offense.

"Just follow my lead with regards to hitting or staying. But bet any way you want. Once every five hands or so, increase your bet randomly when I don't. Remember, we are all playing together. If we consistently win four out of six hands, we will make money. *Or*, if we win two or three, we can make money as long as the hands we win have the most money on them."

"I say high roller pit," Pete announced. "If you want to act like a big dawg, you have to run with the big dawgs."

So they sauntered over to the big dawg pit which was largely empty save for a few Vegas wannabe slicksters that were spread around a craps table. A few other players sat individually at blackjack tables, happy to take on the casino mano et mano. A couple of them sat stone faced as they lost hand after hand. A couple of others might have been homeless, judging by the clothes they were wearing--torn jeans and ratty t-shirts, with dirty New Balance sneakers. They were likely betting with borrowed money in a desperate effort to make a quick buck and that almost always turned out badly. It was an awful sight to see a grown man in tears after he lost his next six months mortgage payments. They eyed an empty table off to the side and sat down. It was fairly evident pretty quickly that only two of them had a clue as to what they were doing.

"Are you planning on playing?" the dealer asked Heather.

"Yes. Why?"

"Because you need to put a bet out."

"Oh," she responded, embarrassed.

"So what's your name?" Sam asked the dealer.

"Li Wong."

"Then why does your name tag say David?"

"Because the casino thought David sounded friendlier."

"Well I hope you're friendly to us," Sam said as the first cards came out of the deck.

It was a six-deck shoe with a cut card about one and a half decks in. That meant it was more difficult to count cards, but not impossible. Theoretically, all the high cards could be left behind the cut card that signaled the end of a shoe, but that would take an incredible string of bad luck. Besides, playing the entire table was bound to limit the damage somewhat. At least a couple out of the six hands were bound to be decent.

Unfortunately, decent wasn't good enough against Li Wong who pulled back-to-back blackjacks right out of the gate. Six rounds in, out of 36 hands, they had collectively won exactly 4 of them and were down more than three thousand dollars. On the 7th hand, things started to look up. Jim and Aaron had 18's, Tommy a 19, Heather a 20, while Pete and Sam were both on 16. But Li Wong was showing a 6, which was a break card so everyone stayed on their hands. When Li turned over his other card and showed a 9, they liked their chances. When he then turned over an ace for 16 with another card to draw, they could practically smell the money. Only three cards in the deck could beat them overall and only one could beat every one of their hands. Which of course, was the card that came out. The 5 of diamonds was a dagger into their collective hearts.

Tommy was still adding the numbers in his head when Pete exclaimed, "21?! You have got to be fucking kidding me."

"What just happened?" Heather asked as the dealer began sweeping up all of their money.

"We lost again," Aaron said.

"Did you pull that card out of your sleeve?" Sam asked with a grin. He was surprisingly not flustered in the slightest.

"We're down more than three grand," Jim stated. "Maybe we should try something else?"

"Nonsense," Sam said. "We just have to ride it out. Keep your bets low until the cards turn."

"And how will we know when that will be?" Heather asked.

"Well, the cards can't run like this forever," Sam reasoned. But he also knew something they didn't.

Most card counters were caught because they didn't say much, had wandering eyes and irrational betting patterns. But Sam was amazing. He could carry on a conversation with two different people, play his own hand, and still keep a running card tally in his head.

The next ten hands were slightly better and they might have broken even on them. On the eleventh hand, Sam suddenly stacked and shoved $3000 into his betting space. Pete looked at him closely, nodded, and did the same.

"Feeling it?" Jim asked.

"We are due," Sam responded simply.

"I agree, but that's a bit too rich for my blood. I'll bet $300."

Heather followed Jim's bet. Tommy's hand was literally shaking as he bet $2000.

"What the hell," Aaron said as he slid $2000 worth of chips into the center.

The pit boss came suddenly alert now. If they were going to make their money, Sam knew it would need to be on this hand. It was now or never. The cards came out. Sam received two face cards for a 20. Pete got blackjack. Jim had a 15. Heather a 19.

Tommy was pleased to get a 20 as well. Aaron had a face card for his first card, but his excitement disappeared when he saw his second card was a 6. He closed his eyes and hung his head.

But Sam's face betrayed nothing. Even when the dealer's up card was the always nerve-racking 2.

"I'd like to split my cards," Sam said.

The dealer looked puzzled. "Why would you break up a winning hand?" he asked.

"Let me ask you this," Sam said. "Would you double down with a 10 against a 2?"

"Well, sure, but a 10 isn't a winning hand."

"You're right. It's going to be *two* winning hands," Sam said as he doubled his bet behind each of his now split face cards.

"Splitting face cards!" Li Wong yelled to get the pit boss's attention. But Sam already had his attention. Ten low bets in a row and suddenly a table max bet.

The dealer, transformed back to David the Friendly before their very eyes when he turned over two more face cards for Sam. He now had two 20's and a grin as wide as Texas.

All eyes turned to Jim's 12.

"Well, Brutha, you've got the most money on the table. You tell me what you want me to do," Jim said.

"If it were me, I'd stay," Sam answered. "Let David do the heavy lifting."

"Even with two face cards already having come out?"

"Have some faith. David will deliver."

"David has been kicking us in the balls for the last half hour," Jim said. "But ok."

Jim waved his hand over the card to signal he was staying. The other three did as well. It was all up to David the Friendly now. He turned over his down card. It was a face card. Followed by a 4 to get to 16.

"I think I've seen this show before," Pete groaned.

"I can't even watch," Heather whispered.

Tommy could only manage a gulp. There was more money on the table than he had made in the last six months.

David turned the last card slowly, looked at it first, then smiled as he dropped a 6 onto the table. Everyone added the numbers in their head and on their fingers just to be sure before jumping up in celebration.

Everyone except Sam that is. He never doubted it for a minute.

X AND THE WHEEL SPINS ROUND

After David the Dealer paid out $15,100 across the entire table, the pit boss congratulated them all on their good fortune, offered to comp a hotel suite for the night, and extended an invitation to continue to play blackjack for the remainder of the evening in the High Roller pit--for the table minimum.   It was his polite way of banning them from the casino for the remainder of their stay. When Sam asked if that applied to all casino games, the man suggested Roulette as an alternative.

"Roulette??" Pete exclaimed. "That's for old ladies and drunk college kids."

"We are certainly not drunk college kids," Aaron confirmed as all eyes settled on Heather.

"If one of you even so much as smirks at me to imply I am an old lady, I will not hesitate to knock you out cold," she responded.

"Roulette it is," Sam said with a laugh.

"I need a burger or something to eat," Tommy answered.

"Johnny Rockets?" Aaron offered.

"Sold."

"I need a drink," Pete said.

"You can drink for free at the roulette table," Jim replied.

"As much fun as drinking watered down vodka while watching a steel ball roll around sounds, I was thinking more along the lines of the Wolf Den or something with a bit more atmosphere."

Heather didn't even hesitate. "I'll join you if that's ok."

"I guess it's just you and me, brutha," Sam said.

"We just made them a ton of money and the ungrateful bastards ditched us," Sam growled. "Their loss. So here's the deal with roulette..."

"There's a deal with roulette? I thought you just picked a few numbers and hoped the little steel ball landed on one of them."

"There's a strategy for everything. For roulette, we bet $100 on black, odd and the middle column of the board. We also bet $50 on the second and third 12 numbers. Then we throw our cover bets on the inside. Ten dollars on 0 and 00. Plus ten dollars on

1, 3, 7, 9, 10, 12, 14, 16, and 18. And always bet 11, 17 and 20. Those are our big numbers."

"How much are we betting on each spin?" Jim asked.

"$540."

"Isn't that a bit steep?"

"Yeah, but with all the cover bets, the most we could lose on any one hand is $190. But as far as the casino is concerned, we're betting $540 a pop, which gets us major comp points. The whole idea is to tread water until we hit a couple of big numbers."

Sam began throwing chips all over the board. There were soon so many chips out there it looked as though he was about to land an aircraft on it. Once all the bets had been made, the dealer flung the steel ball around the wheel.

"Are you happy?" Jim asked. It was kind of a random question and it appeared to startle Sam.

"With my life?" Sam asked.

"Yeah."

"Of course. Why wouldn't I be?"

"I don't know. I just thought that maybe you'd be a little lonely without your friends and family around."

"My friends are wherever I happen to be.   I've been fortunate to meet some extraordinary people and see some incredible sights over the years," Sam answered. "You know I read somewhere that the average person only experiences about 5% of their life's possibilities. I want to experience at least 20% of them."

"How's that working out for you?"

"Pretty good. I'd say I'm at about 15% right now."

The ball bounced around a few times before settling in one of the grooves.

"Red 27," the dealer exclaimed.

"Damnit. See, that's a loser for us. Just lost $190."

"But aren't you worried you're going to miss out on finding that special person to share your life with?"

"To be honest, I saw you find your soulmate only to lose her. And I saw what it did to you. I guess I figured I'd rather miss out on finding that person, than find them and lose them."

"You know what? You may think I'm crazy, but I wouldn't trade one day with her, for 30 years of extra days without her."

Sam nodded. "Well, maybe one day I'll be fortunate enough to feel that same pain."

"Black 17," the dealer said.

"Yahtzee!" Sam exclaimed. "That's the number we were looking for. But listen, it's difficult for me to regret bicycling through the Swiss Alps with the snow covered tops of the Matterhorn in the background. Or running with the bulls in Pamplona, so scared as they closed in, with the greatest feeling of ecstasy ever once reaching safety. Not to mention sitting in the stadium at the opening ceremony of the '96 Winter Olympics in Lillehammer, before watching as the Bobsled competitors flew past at what seemed like light speed. I attended the Sundance Film Festival in Park City, watching these debut films from unknown directors, drinking with movie stars who only wanted to be treated like regular people. And then I spent six months living in a small Upstate New York town where the most exciting happenings were Sunday night bingo at the local church, and Friday night football at the high school. But out of all the places I've been, I think swimming in a cliffside infinity pool in Santorini hanging over a sea bluer than the bluest blue in your most vivid dreams tops them all. About the only thing missing from my life was being able to share these experiences with my little brother."

"I just thought you found me boring and that's why you were always gone," Jim said.

"Are you kidding? We're brothers. You're my best friend and I would kill to have had you with me experiencing those things. But I also knew you were needed here."

"Needed? By whom?"

"Rachelle for starters. The people you work with. Your friends. And of course, mom and dad. I don't know what they would have done without you in their later years. You've led an amazing life, Jimbo. One I could never have led. Not because it's boring. But because I'm not as good of a person as you are. You're my hero, bud. The way you have lived your life, taking on the responsibilities you did, is what enabled me to live mine. I love you."

"Yeah, you're probably right. I am pretty great," Jim responded, a small grin spreading across his face.

Sam put his arm around him and shook his brother playfully.

***

Heather Palmer was one of those women who grew more attractive as she grew older. Her hair was a bit shorter now than when she was in high school, and she had filled out a bit more, but she still had those soulful puddles of deep brown eyes you could lose yourself in. She had an air of confidence about her, not because she thought she was better than anyone else, but because she was long past the point where she cared what other people thought of her. That only served to make her that much more attractive to men, who were always intrigued by the chase. She had her long legs draped over Pete's lap while they sat in casual conversation on two different chairs at the piano bar, the way one might with someone they had known a bit longer than three hours. He was equal parts uncomfortable and excited at the same time as he debated internally between asking her to move her legs and wanting them to stay right where they were.

"So, Jim is right," Pete said at last.

"About what?"

"It doesn't make much sense that you're single. You've never been married?"

"I was engaged once. But one Christmas, I went down to the furnace room to grab an extra folding chair and walked in on my fiancé and my sister having sex," she explained so matter-of-factly that she could have been giving someone directions.

"Oh my god, that's awful," Pete responded.

"Yeah, it hurt--my fiancé that is--when I kneed him in the balls."

"Did you ever speak to your sister again?"

"We were never that close to begin with, but that certainly didn't help matters much. We see each other at holidays and the sort, but that's about it."

"And did they end up together?"

"Nope. The thing I never understood was why she did it. She's always been one of those girls that could get any guy she wanted. Why him? She inadvertently did me a favor to be honest. The guy's been divorced three times already and is working on number 4."

"Well, there is that, then," Pete chuckled. "The Karma Police always gets its man."

"Yeah. So I guess after that, I didn't really see the point. Sure people set me up all the time, but that only makes me seriously wonder what my so called friends must think of me to set me up with the people they do. A friend of mine keeps trying to get me to try one of those online dating sites, but I don't know. It seems like a kind of creepy way to meet someone."

"Thanks a lot. That's how my wife and I met."

"Seriously?"

"Yeah. I have this thing for really short women, so I went on this dating site for midgets. You'd be surprised at how many little women like a tall guy."

"Uh huh," Heather answered, not really sure how else to respond.

"I'm joking, dumbass. I already told you my wife and I met in college."

Heather burst out laughing. "I hate you. I thought you were kidding, but I didn't want to seem insensitive on the chance you were telling the truth. I've only known you a few hours."

"Met the first day of classes freshman year. She was wearing a white button down with tan shorts, black framed glasses that made her blue eyes look even bigger than they were, and these sneakers with thick white side trims that were a cross between a pair of Chuck Taylor's and Nike boat shoes. She was always dressed stylishly. Her hair full of bounce. Makeup perfect. She must have gotten up two hours before class every day just to do it. Everyone else looked like a little girl compared to her. Every guy wanted her. And she chose me."

"That's pretty impressive. How come?" Heather smiled.

"I had no idea at the time, but now that I look back, I think she thought I had the most potential."

"What do you mean?"

"Think she figured I was most likely to make something of myself. The star athletes were stars there, but only a couple of them would go on to the pros. And even then, they'd peak and eventually flame out by 35, unable to cope with their newfound lack of stardom. I think she figured I had staying power."

"It's not sexy, but it's a reason," Heather laughed. "Besides she was right. You're loaded. So how long have you been married?"

"We *were* married for 17 years."

"Were?"

Pete nodded. "We divorced two years ago.

"Any kids?" she asked.

"Two. A boy and a girl. The boy is in college. The girl is headed to college in the fall."

"You guys got married young."

"Yeah. Seems like a lifetime ago. Like we're talking about two completely different people."

"Well, we do change a lot in our 20's and 30's.   You just have to hope you change together."

Pete nodded as he motioned the bartender to bring another round.

"You trying to get me drunk?" Heather asked.

"I would never. I'm a gentleman," Pete winked.

"Then you'd be the first one I've met in a long time," she responded. "I've got to pee."

He loved how frank and unpretentious she was.   The path to the restroom was narrow with the crowd of people and she had to squeeze past Pete to get there. She seemed to hesitate just a moment as she did, brushing up against him, close enough that their lips were about six inches apart. Their eyes met briefly and they smiled at each other without a word before Pete watched her walk down the corridor and out of sight.

XI   RETURN OF THE BALLBAG

Sam and Jim approached the Waterfall Bar in full celebration, and didn't even notice how closely Pete and Heather were sitting at the bar.

"Just call us the rain makers!" Sam exclaimed.

"You won more money?" Pete asked.

"Not me. *We*."

"How did you manage to win at roulette?"

"Let's just say, if I exchanged the money for singles, our great great grandkids could have front row seats at the strip club of their choosing for the rest of their lives. If I turned it into tens, I could make it rain out here for a week. If we used nickel casino chips, we could fill up a storage unit..."

"You made more money?" Tommy asked and he and Aaron approached.

"*We* made more money."

"You mean you and Jim?"

"I mean all of us. We told everyone we'd stake you and then divide up the profits."

"But we didn't even play roulette," Aaron responded.

"That's ok. I'm feeling particularly benevolent. After all, my little brother is alive."

"How much did you actually make?" Heather
asked.

"Oh, I'd say, roughly, $14,435," Sam said.

"How the hell did you manage that?" Pete wondered, chuckling.

"With a lot of luck," Jim responded.

"C'mon, lets go to the Race Book. We can catch the last races at Los Alamitos out in California," Sam suggested.

Jim shook his head. "My brother, the degenerate gambler."

"Your brother, is a winner. Today at least. And when you catch a hot streak, you ride her til she bucks you, or you don't ride at all," Sam answered.

"Going along with your theme of riding, what the heck do you know about horses?" Pete asked.

"Absolutely nothing, but when the gambling gods are smiling upon you, you go with it."

"I know everything there is to know about horses," Chad interjected. He had appeared out of nowhere. As if he had been dropped upon them by some cruel ancient god sent to ruin their evening.

"Ballllbagggg," Aaron growled under his breath just quietly enough that Chad might not have heard him.

"For example, most of the horses that run at Los Alamitos are quarter horses, which means they run shorter distances," Chad continued. "So when you're betting on them, the ones with the inside position have a big advantage since there is usually only one turn in the race. Some races are run down a straightaway, in which case it doesn't matter. Speed is the only thing that does in that case."

"Is he right?" Pete asked.

"Hell if I know," Sam answered, "but let's find out."

"By the way, there was a bit of a crowd getting out of the parking garage outside the bar," Chad said. "Sorry if I took too long. You guys were already gone by the time I got around front."

"That's because we didn't wait," Aaron said with a grin that made it difficult to tell whether or not he was joking.

Another person might have been insulted, but a ballbag didn't know the difference.

The Race Book was largely quiet at that time of night, with only a few degenerates, along with a handful of people who had already taken a beating playing other casino games and were looking to occupy their time without losing a fortune.

"Quarter horse favorites win more often than typical thoroughbred horses. They're more consistent. The variable is a race around one turn. Then inside position is key. Look at the 7th race for example. The favorite is Helen's Boy at 3-1. Decent horse, and is in the 2 position, which is part of the reason he's the favorite. That's the horse to bet," Chad explained.

"Got it," Sam said, as he made his way over to the betting window.

He returned a moment later sporting a huge smile.

"Did you bet the favorite?" Jim asked.

"I bet the only horse that I could bet," Sam answered, slapping the newspaper into his brother's chest.

Jim looked at it and saw the name circled in red ink. "It's spelled wrong," he said before adding, "and he's 42 to 1!"

"Who's 42 to 1?" Heather asked.

"The horse Sam bet on."

"And the horses have reached the starting gate..." the announcer stated on the full wall television screen above them.

"How much did you bet?" Tommy asked.

"Ten Bens," was the reply.

"A thousand bucks?!" Jim exclaimed.

Tommy spit his beer across the floor.

"What would that pay?" Heather asked.

"Well, there isn't that much wagering on the board, so that bet will likely drop the odds to 38 to 1 or so."

"And that pays how much?" she repeated.

"It won't pay anything, because 38 to 1 long shots don't ever come in in quarterhorse racing," Chad advised.

"But if it did," Heather repeated for a third time before pausing and adding for emphasis, "Ballbag."

Aaron nodded his approval for her use of the word.

"About 39K," Sam said calmly.

Heather then spit her beer across the floor.

"If you guys keep spitting your beer out, we're going to end up using all of our winnings replacing the carpeting in here," Sam continued.

"Have you lost your mind?" Jim asked.

"We're playing with house money at this point. Everyone's going home a winner no matter what happens in this race. Besides, making 29K at the casino is a nice story, but making 68K is a legendary one," Sam explained with a wink.

"The last horse to enter the gate is Riley's Wake. He's going off at 38 to 1 odds," the announcer continued as a roar rose up in the Race Book at the mention of the horse's name.

"It's spelled wrong," Jim re-stated matter-of-factly.

"Tis but a moment," Sam said wistfully as the horses broke from the gate.

"And away they go! Helen's Boy and Born to Run both break well and move to the front as they near the first and only turn of the race. Moving well along the outside, but with some ground to make up is Riley's Wake. The horses come around the bend and head for home. It's Born to Run and Helen's Boy. Two hundred yards away. Born to Run and Helen's Boy. And now here comes Riley's Wake! Born to Run.

Riley's Wake. One hundred yards to the wire. And Riley's Wake is making his move. Riley's Wake. Born to Run. And at the wire......sorry Springsteen, it's Riley's Wake by a nose!"

A raucous collective scream rose up from the room, so loud that people began to peer in from outside to see what the ruckus was all about. Even Chad managed a chuckle and a smile. Three thousand miles away from where the race was run, six people, connected solely by one allegedly dead person, were piled in a heap in the middle of the otherwise empty room.

XII   SPIN THE BOTTLE KARAOKE

Jim had been a fan of the Counting Crows since the Northern California band burst onto the music scene in the mid-90's. *Round Here* was his favorite song, but after listening to Chad's karaoke rendition of it, he wasn't sure if he'd be able to listen to either the song or the band ever again.

"*Step out the front door like a ghost into a fog, where no one notices the contrast of white on white...*"

"How is it that intelligent people cannot grasp how awful their singing voice really is?" Jim groused while they all sat around a table in the middle of the bar.

A common trait of a Ballbag was they didn't need to be coaxed on stage. They raced up first as if everyone should be so grateful they were willing to share their talents with the world. The pub wasn't overwhelmingly crowded yet, but the clubs were beginning to close, and the bar would soon be filled by drunk aspiring singers who all had one thing in common--with very few exceptions, they'd be awful. Alcohol didn't help their voices, but it did at least dull the pain of those forced to listen to them.

As Chad the Giant Ballbag tortured the ears of the bar's constituents, Sam decided on a game of his own. He chugged down the last drops of his Corona and slammed it down on the table.

"Here we go. Time for Spin the Bottle Karaoke," he said. "I'll spin this bottle and whichever two people it points to, need to go on stage to sing. Kissing them is optional."

"Count me in," Chad said as he returned to his seat.

"You've done quite enough already," Aaron assured him.

"Was I that bad?" he asked.

Heather, not one for subtlety, answered, "You were awful. Simply awful. The only thing worse was when Aaron relieved himself of gas earlier in the night."

Chad shrugged. "It sounded good from the stage."

"It wasn't," Heather assured him.

"Ok, so here we go," Sam continued, as he readied to spin the bottle. "Jimbo. You still with us?"

But Jim was fixated on the stage at the next singer. She was actually quite good. But even more than that was her song of choice.

"Every time we say goodbye, I die a little. Every time we say goodbye, I wonder why a little. Why the gods above me, who must be in the know. Think so little of me, that they allow you to goooo...."

"I'll be back in a minute," Jim said. "I'm going
to get another round of drinks."

"That's what the waitress is for," Sam answered. "A round is on the way."

"Then I've got to go to the bathroom...or something," he mumbled as he walked away.

"This was the song they played at Rachelle's Wake," Aaron explained to the puzzled group.

***

Rachelle and Jim had dated for two years before he proposed to her on the ferry to Nantucket one July afternoon. Nantucket was about as far from Connecticut as he traveled. No planes involved. Able to make it back home within a few hours if need be.

He always joked that if she had said "no", he was planning to push her overboard. But she said "yes" and they lived a great life together. Both were successful, independent people whose time apart while they were working, only served to make them cherish their time together even more. They had a little tradition they followed whenever she needed to leave on a business trip. Rachelle was a fan of older music. She was a self professed old soul in a young body. She loved the music of her parents; maybe because it reminded her of them. Bobby Darin. Johnny Mathis. Frank Sinatra. Tony Bennett. Etta James. Her favorite was the Cole Porter written song sung by Ella Fitzgerald--"Every Time We Say Goodbye". Jim, in contrast loved more modern music. Maybe it was because he spent most days around teenagers. Maybe it was because he refused to accept the aging process. But when Annie Lennox did a cover of "Every Time..." they found their middle ground and it became their song.

Every time Rachelle would get ready to leave for a work trip, Jim would play the Lennox version, and dance with his wife. He did it as a joke at first, but eventually, it became tradition, and it never failed to bring tears to her eyes.

When she passed away, it was the song Jim had on a continuous loop during the wake. After that day, he never played the song again.

***

"Everything ok?" Sam asked as Jim returned to the table.

"Everything is fine," he replied unconvincingly.

"All right then. Here we go," he said as he spun the empty beer bottle on the table. Around and around it went until it slowly settled to a halt with one end pointing at Sam and the other at Jim.

"Looks like it's you and me, little brother."

"There is *zero* chance that Jim is going to get on that stage," Aaron laughed.

Jim looked directly at Sam and said simply, "I get to pick the song."

"You've got a deal," Sam answered, hopping up from his chair quickly, so as not to give Jim time to change his mind.

There was a delay for some pointing, shuffling, flipping of pages and laughing on the stage as they discussed Jim's choice.

"What do you think they're going to sing?" Aaron asked.

"If I had to guess, something by the Police. Maybe Prince," Pete answered.

The lights dimmed and Sam took the lead vocals while Jim stood with his back facing the audience in the background. The opening chords were immediately recognizable, but they just couldn't believe Jim would ever choose the song. But there was no disputing it once Sam began to sing the opening verse.

"I hopped off the plane at LAX with a dream and my cardigan. Welcome to the land of fame excess. Am I gonna fit in?"

"No. Fucking. Way," a stunned Tommy uttered.

"Can't say I expected this," Heather added.

"I've got to record this," Aaron laughed as he reached for his phone.

"That's when the taxi man turned on the radio and a Jay-Z song was on. And a Jay-Z song was onn! And a Jay-Z song was onnnn!"

At that moment, Jim turned around and stepped forward from the shadows with his arms raised in the air, *"So I put my hands up, they're playing my song, the butterflies fly away! Nodding my head like yeahhh...Moving my hips like yeahhh,"* Jim sang the chorus, swinging and swaying his head and hips to match the music.

Maybe it was the sight of two men approaching 50 singing Miley Cyrus. Maybe it was the irrepressible catchiness of the song itself. Maybe it was that alcohol poisoning had begun to set in to the club crowd that had recently entered the pub. But the place exploded and a hundred people rushed the dance floor, all with their arms in the air.

When the last strains of Party in the USA had faded into the background, the crowd burst into a rousing cheer. Jim waded through the masses back towards the table high-fiving the 20 somethings that were offering their congratulations like he had just scored the winning touchdown in the Super Bowl.

"That was awesome. Simply awesome," Pete said as he gave him a hard high-five.

"Thanks, man. It was either that or Let's Go Crazy by Prince."

"Can't go wrong with either," Pete nodded.

Sam spun the bottle again. "Let's see who's next."

This time, the magic bottle settled on Pete and Heather.

"All right, Sonny and Cher. You're up," Sam informed them.

"Fine," Heather said.

"Fine," Sam answered.

"FINE," she reiterated.

"Don't put too much pressure on yourself," Jim winked. "We're a tough act to follow."

The familiar guitar twang began in the background. After about twenty seconds, Pete began to sing.

"Roll. Won't cha come roll with me. Slow. Fast. Full speed. Girl, wherever sweet time takes us. Hang, with me down this old road, only god knows where we'll go. It don't matter as long as I've got your love..."

Heather joined in at the chorus. *"I don't ever want to wake up, looking into someone else's eyes. Another voice calling me baby, from the other end of the phone...."*

"Tim McGraw. And they don't sound that awful," Jim said.

Sam nodded in agreement.

"You think they're better than I was?" Chad asked.

"Yes!" all four of them at the table said in unison.

"Are you seeing what I'm seeing?" Aaron asked Jim.

"Slide. Slide over nice and close. Lay your head down on my shoulder. You can fall asleep, I'll let you dream..." Pete continued as Heather leaned her head on his shoulder.

"If what you're seeing is our old married friend becoming hot for teacher, then yes," Jim agreed.

The song ended with Pete and Heather inches apart from each other. When they kissed, the bottle of beer Jim was holding, slipped out of his hand onto the floor and shattered.

XIII THE MATCHMAKER

*"C*an I talk to you a minute?" Jim asked Pete once he had returned to the table. He motioned with his head to follow him to the other side of the room.

"Sure."

"Sam clearly stated that kissing was optional. What the hell are you doing?"

"What do you mean?"

"What do you mean what do I mean? You're married."

"Yeah. About that. I'm not actually," Pete acknowledged.

"Not married?"

Pete shook his head.

"What happened?"

"Corrine slept with our son's 25 year old, English soccer coach."

Jim shook his head in disbelief. "Whaaat??"

Pete nodded. "It's true. I mean it's partly my fault. I was traveling a lot for work and I'm sure this guy came along and gave her some attention."

"That is not an excuse, my friend. And certainly not your fault. Is she still with him?"

"Nah. He dumped her a few weeks later for someone closer to his age that could help him get
a green card."

"Serves her right."

"I guess. You know something crazy? I probably would have taken her back if she wanted to come back."

"Are you high? Why on earth would you take her back?" Jim asked incredulously.

"Kind of a moot point, because she didn't want to come back. She said the experience freed something up inside her and she didn't want to be married anymore."

"Jesus. I don't know what to say. How did I not know about this? How did you not tell me?" Jim asked.

"I did call you. A couple of times. But you never called me back, and it wasn't the kind of news I wanted to leave on your voice mail. *'So listen, Corrine and I are getting a divorce. Apparently, she decided she needed to sleep with our son's soccer coach. Hope all is well with you.'*"

Jim ran his hand over his chin in reluctant admittance. "I have been a self-absorbed, self-pitying prick of late."

"I hadn't really noticed a difference to be honest," Pete smiled.

"Very funny. I'm serious. I know I have been."

"We all understand why. You lost the love of your life."

"So did you. Mine died. But yours left you. Might be worse."

"Are you trying to cheer me up, or make me feel worse?" Pete asked.

"Well, I was going for cheering you up, but I could see where I might have failed in that effort," Jim responded. "So what now? Chase the girl?"

"What girl? Heather?"

"No. Minnie Driver in *Grosse Pointe Blank*. Yes, Heather."

"She's great. And I'm sure it would be fun for a night...or a weekend...or a lifetime..." Pete answered somewhat wistfully. "But my job is in California. As are my kids. And she lives in Connecticut."

"There is this thing called 'moving'. It has happened before. *There is but one true love, though there may be a thousand imitations. La Rochefaucauld.* You've had a forgery. It's time to get you an original."

"And you are such a man that could get this for me?" Pete asked.

"I can. Good lord, man, how have you managed to survive all these years since college without me?"

"It's a miracle," Pete said dryly.

"Have I not always given you good advice on the female front?"

"Well, there was the time where you convinced me that girl was checking me out at The Linebacker, and sent me over to talk to her. Only to find out her boyfriend was the starting middle linebacker on the football team, and he happened to be playing pool directly behind us, which is why she was looking in our direction."

"Might have been a slight error in judgment on my part in retrospect. In my defense, we were about 15 beers in if I recall," Jim explained.

"We were, and you've always been there for me. From the first day I met you. I've missed you, bud."

Pete hoisted his beer and clinked bottles with Jim.

"I miss you too. I'm sorry it took me dying to bring us back together. Give me ten minutes," Jim said as he nodded in Heather's direction.

She was seated alone at the table. Sam was on the dance floor, entertaining no fewer than three women with his dancing exploits. Chad was dancing near them, hoping for an invitation to join their circle. Aaron and Tommy were at the other end of the bar doing shots with the bartender.

"What are you going to do?" Pete asked nervously.

"Don't you worry about that," Jim answered as he headed for the table.

He spun a chair around to face him and straddled it, facing Heather. The music was loud, which made having a conversation difficult, but not impossible.

"So," he stated simply.

"So," Heather responded.

"Soooo," Jim repeated.

"Soooooo," she answered slowly.

"I see you've become pretty chummy with Pete."

"He's a nice guy."

"Nice? Mr. Rogers was a nice guy. Bill Nye the Science Guy is a nice guy. Pete is a terrific guy. He's good looking, smart, successful, and has this subtle sense of humor that most people miss."

"That's actually my favorite thing about him," she responded. "He makes me laugh."

"So is it going to happen?" Jim asked.

She fidgeted with the label on her beer bottle. "Is what going to happen? Pete and I? He lives in California. He has teenage children. And his job is one of the reasons his marriage failed."

"Two negatives make a positive," Jim offered.

"That's actually three negatives."

"Then find a fourth one and you'll have a positive," he smiled.

"I don't know. I've known him for all of eight hours. Besides, I had just accepted the fact that I would be spending the rest of my life alone," she said.

"Alone. With a really nice ass and perfect tits."

"Exactly," she laughed.

"Seems like kind of a waste to me. Look. Life throws everyone a curve ball or two. When it does, you can either watch it break over the plate for a strike. Or you can roll with it, and hit it to the opposite field for a home run."

"Home run? I haven't even gotten to second base in over five years."

"Are we still using my baseball metaphor?" Jim asked. "Or did you just tell me you haven't been felt up in five years?"

"*More* than five years," she answered with a smirk.

"Well, I'm fairly certain there would be a plethora of gentlemen who would be more than happy to take care of that for you."

"I'm sure there would be. Because guys are dirtbags."

"Not all guys. Pete, for example, is a stand up guy."

"Are you his agent or something?"

Jim shrugged. "I'm his friend."

Almost on cue, Pete arrived at the table. "Am I interrupting?" he asked.

"Not at all," Jim said. "I was just headed to break the seal."

They both watched him walk away in silence.

"Did he use La Rochefaucauld and his baseball metaphors with you?" Pete asked.

"Yup. He was kind of corny," she answered.

"Yeah. I like him a lot, too," Pete said as Heather slid her hand underneath his and clasped his fingers.

XIV   A FRIEND IN NEED

Aaron had joined Sam, Heather and Pete on the dance floor. Chad was there as well, dancing in all his awkwardness, with arms and limbs flailing in every direction in no particular order. The Irish pub was in full bloom as the hour pushed towards 2:00am.

Tommy stood like the cheese--alone-- drinking a beer at the far end of the bar as Jim approached him.

"Hey, George Thorogood. Why so glum, chum?" Jim greeted him.

"I've had kind of a rough week," Tommy answered.

"Yeah? How so?"

"Well, for starters, I thought the guy who had been like a father to me had died."

"Father?   I ain't that old, bitch," Jim responded defensively.

Tommy laughed out loud. "Ok, uncle."

"Try again."

"Big brother?"

"That's a little more like it. And I'm not dead, so what else happened?"

"Eh, Sheryl's not speaking to me."

"What'd you do?"

Even men knew that when there was an issue between a husband and wife, it was nearly always caused by something the man did.

"Do you remember Tone?"

"The wide receiver on the football team your senior year?"

Tommy nodded. "Yes."

"So what happened?"

"He's been running with a gang and he's been arrested a few times for minor things. But this week he was arrested for dealing within 500 yards of a school. They set his bail at 50 grand, so he called me."

"What about a bail bondsman?"

"They wouldn't touch him. Too much of a flight risk. Anyway, he told me he was a sitting duck in jail. In addition to losing a ton of drugs when he was arrested, they were worried he'd turn on them. So I needed to get him out."

"You have that kind of money?" Jim asked, surprised.

"I did. But on my way to the jail, I was robbed by a fake cop. Lost it all. And now Sheryl isn't speaking to me."

"She's mad because you were robbed?"

"She's mad because I lost our kids' college money. According to her, Tone has made some bad decisions. He made his bed and needs to sleep in it."

"That's understandable," Jim nodded.

"So you think I was wrong to try and help Tone?"

"I didn't say that." "I tried to call her, but I couldn't reach her and needed to act fast," Tommy explained. "Then to top it off, when I couldn't get Tone out, he was beaten in jail and ended up in the hospital anyway."

"Wow. That is a bad week."

"Anyway, she's not speaking to me."

"She'll come around," Jim told him. "Look, it's easy to help someone when there's no sacrifice involved. But making a tremendous sacrifice to help someone. That's the definition of a friend."

"Even when that sacrifice involves my kids?"

"Where do they want to go to school?" Jim asked.

"TJ wants to go to Notre Dame, like his Uncle Jim. I mean, like his big brother Jim," Tommy said, quickly correcting his error. "Jenny is an even better student. She'd love to go to Princeton. But we can't afford either, so UConn it is. Not that we can afford that now either."

"You've got some time. Heck, you made back twelve thousand of it tonight. And you can have my share as well. That gets you halfway there."

"I'm not taking your share. I can't even take my share. I didn't put up the money to begin with."

"Listen. It's not like we're giving you 20 grand. We loaned you 500 bucks and then we all took that money and made more. If it makes you feel better, deduct the original 500, plus 10% interest, which would be outrageously high I might add, and keep the rest. We want you to have it. If you don't take it, we're going to give it to some random stranger here."

"Ok, ok," Tommy relented. "I don't know how to thank you. You've always been there for me, from the very first day we met. Do you remember when that was?"

"Of course I remember," Jim answered. "You had just shanked the potential game winning field goal in the Homecoming game."

"And do you remember what you said to me?"

"You fucking idiot. Now you're never going to get laid."

"Noooo," Tommy laughed. "You came across the field and introduced yourself. Told me you had graduated from Bunnell. And you said no sporting event is ever decided on the last play. It's decided by the 120 plays before it, which, if any one of them had gone differently, might have made the last play meaningless."

"I should have said the first thing. There's more truth to that," Jim lamented.

"You saved my life that day."

"What are you talking about?"

"After the game, no one on my team would even speak to me. My coach gave me a dirty look. And my father, whom I've only met twice in my life, happened to be at that game. He looked at me like I was a loser, so I figured I was. My plan was to go straight to the train station and throw myself in front of the next train."

"That's ridiculous! Nothing is that important."

"Not to us now. But when you're a 17 year old kid, you feel as though the entire world is crumbling around you."

"Good thing you didn't do it, because what happened a month later?" Jim asked.

"I kicked the winning FG in the state championship game," Tommy nodded.

"Exactly."

"I'm glad you're not dead," Tommy chuckled.

"I'm glad I'm not too," Jim answered. "Now go call your wife."

"It's 2:00am. She's sleeping."

"Then you don't know women very well. They can never sleep when they're upset. She'll probably answer on the first ring."

Tommy relented. He dialed her number and hadn't even gotten the phone to his ear before she picked up.

"Hi babe," he said quietly while Jim smiled in the background.

XV THE ADMISSION

It was close to 3:00am by the time the Denali pulled away from the Sky Valet at the casino. Within minutes, most of its passengers were asleep. Heather was lying with her head resting on Pete's lap in the third row of seats, drooling slightly as she slept. Pete fell asleep while gently rubbing her shoulders. Tommy was sleeping as well, a peaceful smile on his face after having patched things up with his wife and armed with the knowledge that his "father/uncle/brother" figure was still very much alive. Sam, he of the endless energy, finally ran out of steam, the emotional swings of the day, the time difference from traveling across the Atlantic, the 15-20 drinks, the gambling, not to mention four hours of dancing, having taken its toll.

Of the passengers, only Jim remained awake, and it was a continuous battle to remain that way. But he was determined not to leave Aaron to make the hour long drive home in the dark by himself.

"Quite a day, huh?" Aaron remarked.

"It was different than I expected. That's for sure," Jim responded. "And I mean that in a good way."

"Biggest surprise?"

"I'd have to say the number of people that showed up. I think we all wonder who would come to our funeral. You assume your family and close friends will, but will you have touched any other lives enough for them to show up?"

"Well, you must have touched quite a few lives then, because the place was packed. The owner asked if we could have another fake wake next weekend."

"They say weddings and funerals are like moving pictures of your life."

"One could argue that weddings and funerals are one and the same," Aaron quipped.

"You're only saying that because your wife isn't around to punch you in the face."

"Damn straight. Favorite moment?"

"A draw between Riley's Wake winning at Los Alamitos, the last hand of blackjack we played, and singing *Party in the USA* at the pub."

Aaron laughed. "I still can't believe you did that."

"My brother has a way of getting people to do things they otherwise would never consider doing," Jim explained. "He got our mother to skateboard down the steep hill on our street when we were kids. He convinced Mike Mancuso to jump off the Sikorsky Bridge when we were 12. But probably his greatest accomplishment was getting Delaney Boyer to play strip poker with a group of us at Rob Ward's party."

"Who was she?" Aaron asked.

"Only the most beautiful girl in the school. Captain of the cheerleading squad. Straight A student. Huge prude. And somehow, Sam had her down to her bra and parties in a room with 150 people. He couldn't get her any further than that, at least not publicly, but I'm fairly certain he got them off in private."

"Person you were happiest to see?"

"Excluding you of course since I went there *with* you, I'd have to say Sam. He has this disarming quality about him, and it doesn't matter how long he's been gone, to get you right back into the old routines in a matter of minutes. Smiling. Laughing. He makes you feel as though you're the most important person in the room. And there's nothing fake about it. But then he's gone again, and you feel like you lost him all over. It's heartbreaking."

"Why don't you go visit him?" Aaron asked.

"I might."

"You should. Person that showed up that you *didn't* want to see?"

Jim shook his head. "I can't really think of anyone."

"C'mon. Even the Giant Ballbag?"

"Chad's ok. He's just awkward. Always has been. I'm always amazed at how some really smart people can have no social skills whatsoever. But he means well."

"And what do you make of our budding couple in the back?"

"I think they're cute together. Heather is beautiful, smart and funny. She deserves someone who will treat her well. And Pete is about the most decent person I know. I can't believe I didn't know he was divorced. I have been a real ahole. And I probably owe you the biggest apology for that. You lost your sister. And then you lost your best friend on top of it."

"You're making some giant assumptions with that last part," Aaron smirked.

"Ha. Ha," Jim answered in a sarcastic, measured tone.

"So what's next for you?"

"What do you mean?"

"In life."

"I don't know,' he shrugged. "But I'm looking forward to it, whatever it is."

They sat in silence the rest of the way, each in apparent deep thoughts as they raced past the reflector lights on the otherwise darkened highway, with an occasional car passing by on the other side of the road. They dropped Tommy off first. Jim reached into the back seat and gave him a hearty handshake.

"You good?" Jim asked.

Tommy nodded. "All good," he responded. "See you at work Monday?"

"You can count on it. Give your wife and kids a hug for me."

Heather and Pete were next. They had decided to have a sleepover at her house. Jim got out of the car to help them out of the back.

"Be good to each other," he said. He gave Heather a warm hug. "It was really good seeing you again. We live in the same town for heaven's sake. Don't be such a stranger."

"You don't be a stranger," she replied. "Howard Hughes," she added with a wink.

"Sorry again for dragging you all this way," he said to Pete.

"It was well worth the trip. I'm glad you're ok."

"If you need anything. And I mean, anything, I'm here. And I promise I'll call back."

Pete clasped Jim's hand with one of his giant bear cub paw hands and pulled him in for a man hug.

Asleep the entire time was Sam. When they finally pulled up to Jim's house, Jim leaned into the back and said, "Wake up, Sambo. We're home."

Sam awoke with a start as if he hadn't been sleeping for the last hour and a half. Aaron got out of the car and walked around to say goodbye.

"Great seeing you, Sammy. Hopefully we can do it again soon. Not the wake part, but getting together."

"Most definitely. Aaron. It's always a pleasure, never a chore."

They hugged and then Aaron turned to Jim. "When am I going to see you again?"

"How about brunch tomorrow? Bring the family."

"I'd like that. I'm sorry we never found out who was behind this," Aaron added.

Jim put one hand on each side of Aaron's head and kissed each cheek.   "I know it was you, Fredo. I know it was you."

"What makes you say that?" Aaron asked.

"Because you're the only one who knows me well enough to write that obit. And you're the only friend who would care enough to do it." He paused briefly before adding, "Thank you."

"You're welcome," Aaron answered with a smile.

XVI   A FRESH START

Heather received a thunderous cheer from the kids upon entering her kindergarten classroom. The last day of school was always bittersweet. On one hand, summer and sunshine were waiting with open arms to greet all who had put in a rightful shift for the better part of the past ten months. On the other, it was difficult saying goodbye to those you had grown close to over that same amount of time.

"I'm going to miss you, Miss Palmer!" a little girl shouted as she ran over and gave her a hug by wrapping her tiny arms around Heather's legs.

"I'm going to miss you too," Heather answered.

"But not more than peanut butter," the girl clarified. "That's my favorite and my mom lets me eat more of it during the summer because she doesn't have time to make big lunches."

"I love peanut butter too," Heather laughed.

While most of the kids played together, there was one boy seated by himself on the other side of the room. Any teacher will publicly say they don't have favorites, but it's a lie. Their favorites were always those kids that showed up on time, were respectful to others and worked hard. Darren Gallagher had short hair, more straight than wavy, dimples in both cheeks, and was always perfectly dressed for any occasion. He was the boy who always did exactly what was asked of him. The boy who would place his mat during nap time next to the person no one else wanted to lie next to. The boy who would stop whatever he was doing to help someone who had spilled something, without you even having to say anything.

"What's wrong?" Heather asked as she approached him.

The boy looked up at her with his piercing blue eyes and said steadily, "The school year is over and that means I'm not going to get to see you anymore."

"It's summertime! You can play with all your friends," she asserted.

"But you're my best friend," he wailed.

She had to choke back her tears. "You're my best friend, too. Just don't tell the others."

"But I'm not going to get to see you," the boy sniffed.

"That's the thing about best friends. They don't have to see each other every day to stay best friends. And when they do see each other--well, that makes it even more special," she explained.

"How come?"

"Look at it this way. What kind of cereal do you like?"

"Apple Cinnamon Cheerios is the best, he exclaimed proudly.

"Ok. And if you ate that every single day, eventually, you'd get sick of it, wouldn't you?"

"I don't knowww. It's really good."

She laughed. "It is really good. But I bet if your mom didn't let you eat it for a few days, you'd be really excited when you got to eat it again."

"If my mom didn't let me eat it for a few days, I'd be real mad. But then I'd be excited."

"That's kind of how best friends are. They're like Cheerios. You love them and you miss them when they're not around, but you get really excited when you get to see them again."

"Am I going to get to see you again?" Darren asked innocently.

"Of course you are. I promise to visit."

When the bell rang to signal the end of the school day, Heather walked her students out to the buses and their parents waiting cars before returning to her classroom. She packed up her personal items and placed them in an open cardboard box. Pencils. Pens. Markers. Paste. Scissors. All weapons of choice for a kindergarten teacher. She added two pictures that had been made for her by her students and put the lid back on.

Carrying the box with her arms stretched out in front of her, Heather paused in the doorway of the only place she had spent more time over the past twenty years than her home, before pulling it closed behind her for the last time.

Her apartment was filled floor to ceiling with boxes, each taped closed and neatly labeled. Two suitcases on wheels stood at the ready with their handles extended, waiting for the honk of the horn that would signal her ride was there. When it came, Heather leaned out the window and waved at Jim, who signaled he was coming up to help her with her luggage.

He carefully loaded the bags in the back of his SUV and slid into the drivers seat.

"What kind of spaceship looking thing is this," Heather asked.

"*This*...is the Maserati of SUVs," Jim answered.

"I thought you always bought American?"

"Not always," he said. "Now do you have everything you need? Toothbrush and toothpaste?"

"Check."

"Jacket for those cool evenings?"

"Check."

"Underwear?"

"Don't wear it. Don't need it."

"Excuse me?" he said, eyebrows arched.

"I'm kidding. Yes, dad, I have everything I need. And if I don't, we can buy it out there."

"Ok then. We're off."

An hour later, he pulled curbside in front of the United Airlines check in. He handed her bags over to one of the agents along with a twenty dollar bill.

"I'll make sure the rest of your things and your car make it on the moving van Monday."

"I can't thank you enough."

"It's not a problem. You take care of yourself.

Safe travels," he said as he hugged her goodbye.

Heather was feeling a plethora of emotions as the plane soared over the Statue of Liberty and headed west. Excitement. Nervousness. Happiness. Even sadness. She welcomed change in her life, but calling a new place home was a bit disconcerting nonetheless. She hadn't left Connecticut for more than five days in a row her entire life, and hadn't left it at all in five years. Even so, home wasn't a destination. It was wherever your heart was.

She listened to some music and had a couple of drinks to calm her nerves. Then enjoyed a meal and watched a movie to pass the time. Five and a half hours later, the plane touched down on the runway.

"United Airlines and this New York based flight crew would like to welcome you to San Francisco, where the local time is 10:11pm," the stewardess said upon arrival at the gate.

Heather was normally a model of decorum, but at that moment, was being driven by excitement. She elbowed her way past a few elderly people and two little kids to get off the plane. Her walk would be more accurately described as a gallop as she made her way down the ramp. She exploded through the double doors that led to the terminal and scanned the immediate area. Her eyes finally settled on her reason for being there.

Pete waved and she tried to approach him casually, even though her heart was racing and felt like it might explode through her shirt at any moment. When she was about ten feet away, both of them threw casualness out the window. She ran into his arms and he lifted her into the air, spinning her around as he kissed her.

"Welcome home," he said as he placed her back on the ground.

XVII   SOMETIMES DREAMS DO COME TRUE

Jim was sifting through some papers on his desk when Tommy entered the office.

"So what did TJ decide for college? Is he going to be a Fighting Irishman?" Jim asked casually.

"He's actually going to stop by here in a few minutes to talk about it. But I just don't see how we can swing it."

"No?"

"With all the overtime you've let me work, I've got our college savings back up to just over 60 grand. But it's not enough."

"What are the costs?"

"Notre Dame is nearly 60 grand a year. He qualified for a $15,000 academic scholarship, and we got 20K in need based aid.   But it still leaves 25K a year left," Tommy explained.

"But you just said you've got 60K saved," Jim responded.

"I do. But college is four years and we've got Jenny coming along in two years."

"A lot can happen in two years," Jim said.

"A *whole* lot would need to happen," Tommy laughed. "If they both go to UConn, it will cost us 10 grand a year. That's 80 grand total for both of them. And it gives me 5 years to come up with the other 20 grand. The kids can take out a student loan to cover incidental expenses and only have twenty thousand in loans when they graduate."

"Makes sense," Jim nodded. "But ND's got a huge alumni network. He could write his own ticket coming out of there. And you said Jenny is Ivy League caliber."

"She is. And if we were loaded or poverty level, we'd be able to send them wherever they wanted to go. But we make just enough money that we can't swing it. Crazy world we live in, isn't it?"

"Tell you what. Rachelle and I never had any kids. Your kids are like our kids. I've got some extra money lying around. Why don't you let me cover the difference?"

"I'm not going to let you pay for my kids' college. You've done enough for us."

"I had a feeling you'd say that," Jim answered. "Ok, how bout this? I *loan* the money to your kids and they can start paying it back when they get their first job. Some nominal amount spread out over thirty years.

I'll probably be dead long before that, at which point, they would be absolved."

"I don't even know what absolved absolved means," Tommy said.

"It means when I die, they no longer owe anything."

"Look, Jim, I appreciate it. I really do. Can't even begin to tell you how much. But you've done enough for us over the years."

"I had a feeling you'd say that too. Ok, then," he relented. "By the way, here's your direct deposit receipt. Might want to double check it. A couple of people have said their checks hadn't hit their account yet."

Tommy opened the envelope and looked inside. Casually at first, then with laser-like focus. It was at that exact moment, that his son walked in. Classically good looking with well-chiseled features and a welcoming smile, he was the spitting image of his father.

"Hi Jim. How are you," he asked as he went over to shake his hand.

"I'm good, TJ. Everyone treating you ok on your summer job?"

"Definitely," he answered. "Thank you for setting it up for me."

"I'm only hearing good things, so thank *you*. Sort out your college decision yet?" Jim asked.

"Actually yes," TJ answered. "Pop, I know you wanted to talk about schools, but I've made up my mind. I want to go to UConn. I figure that way I can bring my laundry home on the weekends, and it won't stress you guys out financially. Plus, Jenny's an even better student than I am, so maybe she can go somewhere better."

"That's a really mature and unselfish way of looking at things," Jim said. "Don't you think so, Tommy?"

But Tommy's fingers were typing as furiously on his computer keyboard as it would let him. He looked down again at the deposit receipt and then at his bank account balance on the computer screen. It read, $760,067.27. That was after taxes had been taken out of a *million* dollars.

"Dad? Everything ok?"

"I'll be back in a minute. Talk to Jim," Tommy said distractedly as he ran from the room.

"What the heck was that all about?" TJ asked.

"I have no idea," Jim said, fighting back a sneaky broad smile.

When Tommy approached the personnel director with his discovery, he was informed that it was not a mistake. The same anonymous donor who had donated a million dollars to complete the field project renovation at the middle school, had donated a million dollars to the man who had taken care of it for the past fifteen years. Tommy fell to his knees and began sobbing. He had always been a sensitive man, but this time, he was crying tears of joy.

Six weeks later, Tommy packed up his SUV and he and TJ made the twelve hour drive to the University of Notre Dame. They drove past the black and gold marble entrance sign, past the stone and ivy covered buildings and past the library with the mural of Jesus on the side of it. It was known as "Touchdown Jesus" for having his arms raised in the air, and being located just beyond the end zone of famed Notre Dame Stadium.

Tommy had no idea that the man who had made it all possible, was the same man he had shared an office with for the past fifteen years. He knew that Jim didn't need to worry about where his next meal was coming from, but he never knew how wealthy he actually was. Jim wrote his books under a pseudonym. Not to mention most of his friends and co-workers would never considered "avid readers". And with the possible exception of his recent purchase of a Maserati, Jim had never been flashy with his money.

TJ got out of the car in complete awe of his surroundings. And the sight of his son so happy might have been the most beautiful sight Tommy's eyes had ever seen.

XVIII THE ROAD LESS TRAVELED

Jim's internal alarm woke him up from a light sleep about two minutes before his clock was about to ring. On the surface, it seemed like any other day, but the energy he had about him implied something different.

He asked Alexa to play Tim McGraw and she obliged by shuffling and playing some of his songs while he showered. Khakis and a v-neck sweater was his uniform, and he had five or six sets of each, which made choosing an outfit fairly straightforward. He poured himself a glass of orange juice to go along with his two slices of potato bread toast that were smothered in butter and followed by taking his morning multi vitamin.

Jim pulled up to the drive thru window at Dunkin Donuts and ordered the usual. Four large coffees. Black. Black with two sugars. Light and sweet. And an iced coffee. They were for the facilities crew at Park and

Rec, the men who made him look good at his job, and the tradition had started 10 years ago when he brought them coffee before asking them for a huge favor. It continued for no other reason than he liked the guys.

"Gentlemen," Jim said, "and I use that term loosely. Your morning coffee."

"I can't believe you're leaving us," one of the men said.

"Only for a month," Jim responded.

"Does that mean we are going to have to get our own coffee?" another one asked.

"You guys don't even care that I'll be gone. You just want free coffee."

"Obviously," the first one answered with a laugh.

"Don't worry about it. It's been taken care of," Jim said with a wink.

It was a rarity that Tommy beat Jim into the office, but he was already there on this morning, with his feet up on Jim's desk.

"Your desk really is much nicer, and you've got a better view," Tommy said.

"Don't get used to it. Because I'm reclaiming it upon my return," Jim stated. He reached into a folder and removed a sheet of paper that he handed to Tommy. "Here's the list of can't mess up things. Don't screw them up."

"*Number 1. Morning coffee for the facilities guys. Black. Black with two sugars. Light and sweet. And an iced coffee,*" Tommy read from the sheet. "*Number 2. Call the school athletic directors each morning to make sure there are no changes to the schedule. Then confirm with facilities. Number 3. When the kids arrive for youth pickup basketball in the afternoon, pull the best player aside (you know the kids) before they choose teams and have him select the weakest player first. Tell him it will make him a better player and show signs of leadership. Number 4. Don't forget to introduce the lineups for the nighttime adult volleyball leagues with music. They love it. Number 5 and most important. Leave out two blueberry donuts and an orange juice for the nighttime cleaning lady. Geez. It's* not going to be easy being you."

"Maybe not at first, but you'll figure it out before I get back," Jim smiled.

"Are you sure you're coming back?"

"And give up all this?" Jim asked with his arms wide. "Of course I'll be back."

"Well, if you change your mind, can I have your Maserati?"

"You got it."

"Would you mind putting that in writing?"

"Now, you're pushing it."

A couple of hours later, Jim found himself bellied up to an airport bar waiting for his overnight flight. On one side of him was a married couple arguing about how much money they had recently spent on home improvements.

"I don't mind doing some improvements, but we can't do them all at once. Hardwood floors. Kitchen addition. New backsplash."

Arguing over money. 75% of married couples' arguments stemmed from money. 15% from one or the other either giving or receiving in private areas of their body that should have been off limits to outsiders. And 10% because, well, people loved to argue.

Seated to Jim's left was an attractive brunette woman, about 40, casually but nicely dressed.

"So did they strip search you too? Or was it just me?" Jim asked.

The comment could have gone one of two ways. It could have served as an icebreaker. Or it could have resulted in a dirty look with no response whatsoever.

"Three times actually," the woman responded. "Which I thought was a bit of overkill. But I took it as a compliment."

"Hard to blame them if you walked up after I did," Jim laughed. "I'm Jim."

"Stephanie. Nice to meet you."

Her boarding pass was sticking out of her purse on the bar. Jim tried to be subtle about reading it, but wasn't very good at it.

"You're headed to Athens as well?" he asked. "Vacation? Or do you live there?"

"Visiting my grandparents," she answered. "What about you?"

"I'm actually only flying into Athens, before heading to Santorini to visit my brother."

"He lives there?"

"For now he does. You could say he's a bit of a free spirit," Jim said in the understatement of the year.

"And what do you do?" she asked. "Stockbroker? Hedge fund guy?"

"Do I look like either of those?" Jim asked.

"You're actually hard to place. Neat and clean. Sharply dressed but not showy. You have money, but don't advertise it."

"I'm a writer."

"For a magazine?"

"Books."

"Get out," she said, not sure if she believed him. "I own a small bookstore in Fairfield."

"Aren't many of those left. I live two towns away in Stratford."

"We focus mostly on self-published authors and independent publishing houses. We have book clubs and book signings. You write anything I might know?"

"The Shady Badesso Chronicles?"

"You're Conner Steele?"

"Jim Reilly actually. But Conner Steele is my pen name."

"Would you consider doing a signing at my store?" she asked hopefully.

"I usually try to keep a pretty low profile," Jim said.

"I can't think of much more low profile than my store," she laughed.

"Sure. I'll do it. But now you're going to have to give me your number," he said, after glancing at her wedding finger to make certain it was barren.

"You do the signing, I'll even let you take me to dinner."

"What makes you think I'd want to do that?" Jim smiled.

"Who are you trying to kid? You were staring at me from the moment you walked in, and waited until there was an empty seat next to me, instead of taking the open one a few seats down. Women notice everything. We just pretend that we don't."

"I was actually looking at the TV behind you that had the game on I wanted to see," Jim said. "The people where the empty seat was were watching another game."

Stephanie wheeled around and saw the basketball game over her shoulder. "Oh. Don't I feel stupid?"

"Not at all," Jim smiled.

"Now boarding our First Class passengers for Flight 2287 to Athens through Gate 62," the announcement blared.

"That's me," Jim said, standing up. "What's your number?" he asked.

She reached into her purse and handed him a business card. Jim handed her one of his. She looked puzzled.

"This says, *Town of Stratford Park and Recreation Director*."

"That's where I work when I'm not writing. And most of the people there don't know I write. I'd prefer to keep it that way."

"Well, aren't you a mysterious man," she smiled. "Have a safe flight. I'll see you in baggage claim. By the way, I hope you packed lightly, because if you're taking a boat into Santorini, there's only two ways up the mountain--cable car or a donkey. And neither is very conducive to carrying a lot of luggage."

"Backpack and duffle bag," Jim smiled. "And I'm flying in. So I probably won't see you in baggage claim."

He stopped by the counter at the gate before boarding the plane. "Question for you. When I was checking in for the flight last night, it looked like the seat next to me in First Class was open. Is that still the case?" Jim asked.

"It is," the attendant answered bruskly. She was clearly a bit rushed as people lined up to board the plane.

"Would it be possible to upgrade a passenger friend of mine from the main cabin?"

"That is done based on airline miles," she responded.

"How about if I buy the upgrade? Her name is Stephanie Gianopolis," he said, handing the agent a credit card.

She was annoyed, but took it nonetheless.

"One more thing," Jim said. "Don't tell her I bought the upgrade. Just tell her it was a random one."

Jim had just nestled into his seat when a familiar and welcome face appeared.

"Well, well, well," she said. "I guess you're not the only one who's special."

"Miss Gianopolis," Jim answered, feigning horror. "Are you stalking me?"

"You wish. Free upgrade. Make sure you keep your arm on your side of the arm rest."

And then she smiled. Jim couldn't have explained it if you gave him a year's worth of Sunday's to try, but there was something about her he was drawn to. She was pretty, yes, but there were plenty of pretty women. Near as he could tell, it had something to do with the lilt of her voice. He had read somewhere that a person's voice could trigger pheromones that made the other person seem incredibly attractive to them. He had always thought it was bunk, but as he looked directly into her saucer wide brown eyes, suddenly he wasn't so sure anymore. Unfortunately, further analysis would need to wait because he had other immediate plans.

They begrudgingly said their goodbyes in baggage claim, and left open the possibility of her visiting the island for a day or so while she was in Greece. If not, there would certainly be time for a reunion back in Connecticut.

Jim attached his backpack by wrapping it over both shoulders. Comfort and ease trumped style, especially when he also had a duffle bag and laptop to carry. The flight into the island was about 45 minutes from Athens, with breathtaking views on the approach. He likened it to landing on an aircraft carrier, with the airport runway perched on one of the only completely flat areas on the entire island.

The bright sunshine left him a bit disoriented as he made his way down the steps of the plane onto the ramp. His body was telling him it was 3:00am, but his eyes were telling him something completely different. As he entered the terminal, Sam was there to greet him, with his arms wide as if to say, "Now do you understand?"

They hugged and Sam grabbed Jim's duffle bag before they jumped in a waiting car for transport to the hotel where Sam lived and worked.

"We're headed to Oia," he said.

"How's that spelled?" Jim asked.

"O-I-A. But it's pronounced Eee-AH."

"That's like saying our last name is Reilly but it's pronounced Larow," Jim said.

Sam laughed. "Hence the phrase it's all Greek to me."

The entrance to the hotel was a non-descript, tall white wall surrounding a matching gate. But once they stepped inside the grounds, Sam's life suddenly made sense to Jim. The whitewashed buildings surrounded an infinity pool that appeared to drop off into the Aegean Sea some three hundred feet below. A glance to the west showed the blue domed rooftops of a couple of churches in the village and the curve of the volcano showed the far end of the island in the distance.

"What do ya think?" Sam asked.

"I think I'm a writer and never in a million years would I be able to find the words to adequately describe this," Jim answered.

"It is amazing, isn't it?"

"Two roads diverged in a wood, and I--I took the one less traveled by. And that has made all the difference," Jim recited.

"Robert Frost."

Jim nodded. "I now understand why you've lived the life you've lived."

"Like I said, the only thing missing from it was the opportunity to share it with my brother. Thanks for coming."

"Thanks for being so persistent," Jim responded.

"Well, Rachelle wouldn't have allowed for anything less."

Jim titled his head with a cocked eyebrow, confused.

"She sent this to me not long before she died," Sam said as he held out a handwritten note.

"*Sammy boy,*" Jim read. "*Although we haven't gotten to spend a lot of time together over the past fifteen years, I'd like to think the time we did spend was quality time. And because of that, I know you are the only person who will be able to complete the task I'm assigning you. When I go, and it won't be long now, make certain that Jim remains an active participant in his life. Life was not designed to be a spectator sport. That's grown more obvious to me as I near the end of mine. Now, he will fight you on this every step of the way, but don't give up on him, please don't ever give up, because once you break through, you will be exposed to the kindest and gentlest soul ever created. Of course you know this because he's your brother. Safe journeys, Sammy boy. I look forward to our tearful reunion on the other side of the moon. Love, Shell.*"

Neither said a word when he was finished reading it. They didn't need to. Looking out into the sea through the pools of tears that had formed in their eyes, they saw a boat coming towards the harbor, while another headed away from the island. The passengers on the ships' decks waved at each other. They may have been headed in opposite directions, but each person would have their own distinct journey to make and each, their own distinct story to tell.

AUTHOR'S NOTES

Usually, the title is the last thing I come up with in a story. I normally think of an incident, an idea or a character and then create a story around it. Once I have it pretty well fleshed out, I come up with a title. This is the first book out of the eight that I've written where I reversed that.

I was out for dinner and drinks with a couple of my Scottish friends one night while we chided one of them who can't handle anything spicier than salt, for nursing his hard cider. *A slow drinker* he was. He then affectionately referred to the other as a *ballbag* – the polite description of which is someone who's extremely annoying. As the evening went on, one of us might have passed gas and then been called a *smelly bastard*. We laughed so hard at the title we had created, that I just had to develop a story around it.

Hence, *Slow Drinkers, Giant Ballbags & Smelly Bastards.* In this story, you meet them all, and hopefully you enjoy reading it as much as I enjoyed creating it. Like everything I tend to write, this book is heavy on family, friendship and loyalty – with a little dose of romance thrown in for good measure.

Special thanks to Scott McBride and Rich "Solid" Sutherland for the evening that gave the book its unusual name.

I'll see you all on the other side of the moon.

*Enjoy this book? Turn the page for a glimpse at the critically acclaimed novel about a dying man looking for redemption in the eyes of his son...**The Music Box**...*

I
JOSH~

Josh Reynolds had a perpetual smile on his face, even when he was nervous — which he was at that very moment. He was mid-to-late 30-something, but looked much younger than his age. Nearly always dressed in a pressed, blue Oxford and khakis, on this day, his shirt was unbuttoned at the top and the sleeves were folded up twice on each side. A tie hung loosely around his neck. That was Saturday casual dress at the biggest advertising agency in the world. He hated working weekends like most people hated the dentist, but deadlines were deadlines, and clients didn't differentiate between weekdays and weekends.

He checked his watch as he stepped into the elevator, before he realized he was stepping in front of a woman. He stopped, placed his arm in front of the doors, and waited for her to enter. She smiled at him the way all women did. Didn't matter who they were, women were drawn to his manners, easy charm and clean-cut good looks. They were gifts from his father without him even realizing it.

The door opened on the 2nd floor and a disheveled looking man in his mid-20's stepped on. He looked as though he had been up most of the night. It was all he could do to nod at Josh in acknowledgment.

"Morning, Petey," Josh said. "You ready for the big presentation?"

"I think so," Pete answered with somewhat less confidence than Josh was hoping for.

"Well, let's hear it."

Pete paused, then motioned with his hands as if he was creating a billboard. "Why buy just one, when it might take five to do the trick?"

Josh stared at him in disbelief, his jaw dropping to almost floor level. "You're joking, right?"

"I don't think so," he said sheepishly.

"Petey, we're selling feminine protection here, not breath mints!"

"Well, we thought about going the other way. *Why buy a whole box, when one might do the trick?* But we thought the client might think we were encouraging people to buy less of their product."

"Good thinking," Josh said sarcastically. "Look, your saying will get people thinking about women who have…"

Pete looked puzzled. "Who have what?"

"Who have a heavy…you know."

"Heavy--"

The woman, silent until this point, leaned in. "Flow," she whispered.

"Thank you," Josh nodded before turning back to Pete. "Petey, we need to fix this or Bill's going to have a shit right there in the conference room. I'm going to go stall him. You and Jimbo need to come up with an alternate slogan. And you need to do it fast, because my son's basketball game starts in two hours out in Connecticut."

"I think it might be a little late for that."

"Why??"

"Because Bill sent someone down to pick it up earlier this morning, so he could have an advance look at it."

"And you gave it to him??!!"

"He's my boss," Pete explained.

"I'M your boss!"

"But he's your boss."

"Which is why you should let me deal with him! This is not good. Bill's going to toss us all out of the 11th floor conference room window."

The elevator doors opened, and Josh raced down the hall to Bill Palmer's office. As he approached it, he could already hear Bill yelling from inside.

"Find Josh Reynolds!" Bill screamed at his secretary.

Josh motioned to her to pretend she hadn't seen him and did an abrupt 180 degree turn in the hallway. She just smiled at him. The way all women did.

Five minutes later, Josh slid into a seat next to Pete and Jim in the back of the conference room. There were ten other executives also in attendance. This would not be a pleasant experience he concluded.

"Did he look at the ad?" Pete asked nervously.

"I think it's safe to say that he did."

"Did he like it?"

"Let's just say, I hope your resume is up to date."

Bill entered the room. He was in his early 50's, with a thick head of mostly dark hair, with some grey sprinkled in. He had started as a copywriter twenty-seven years ago and worked his way up to CEO, stopping for a brief time at every rung of the ladder along the way. He was loud, bombastic even, but it was difficult not to respect a man who had actually worked his way to the top instead of having it handed to him.

"Josh," Bill began surprisingly calmly.

"Yes, Bill."

"What are my feelings on hiring morons?"

"You're generally opposed to it," Josh responded matter-of-factly, as if he was stating company policy.

"Exactly. It makes for bad business."

"That makes sense."

"Glad you agree with me. Now explain to me then, knowing how I feel about this, why you would put two morons in charge of one of our most lucrative clients?"

"Poor judgment on my part?" Josh offered, sending a steely look Pete and Jim's way.

"And what do they call the person who hired the two morons?" Bill continued.

"A bigger moron?"

"Exactly. *Why buy one when it might take five to do the trick??* Jesus H, we're not selling Hot Tamales here!"

Josh looked back at Pete as if to say he told him so.

"What's the single most important factor to consider when selling feminine products?" Bill asked. "Jean?"

Jean was in her late 40's, most likely past her tampon usage days. Her eyes grew wide. She wasn't expecting to have to answer any questions. She preferred to work behind the scenes and be neither praised nor yelled at.

"Comfort?" she responded shyly.

"Good. And what else? Josh?"

"Uh, I've never used one, Bill."

"Neither have I," he answered, not missing a beat. "But I've seen them in trashcans. I'm sure you have too. And what's your reaction when you stumble onto one?"

"Eww?"

"Exactly. And what is one of the primary advantages our product offers?"

"Discretion?"

"Bullseye. So let's sell some goddamn discretion then! What I need is for you and the other two morons to sit here until you figure this shit out. Tell your wives you won't be home until you've got a slogan we can pitch. I've got to go see my chiropractor. Text me when you're done."

Josh rose from his seat. He knew it was a poor time to make a stand, but decided to make it anyway. "Bill," he said as he checked his watch, "I've actually got to leave for a while. My son's league championship basketball game starts in forty-five minutes out in Connecticut."

"And I'm sure it will be a helluva game. But he's ten."

"12 actually."

"Fine. He's 12. But don't act like it's the NBA Finals. Take care of this, Josh, because the only thing worse than being the guy who hired two morons is being the guy who hired the moron who hired two morons. Because you know what that makes him?"

"The biggest moron?"

"Exactly. And I have no intention of being the biggest moron."

"I hear ya, Bill. But I still have to leave."

There was a palatable uncomfortableness in the room.

"I wouldn't if you value your job."

"I do. Value my job that is. But I value my son even more. I'll make sure I'm reachable and will stay up all night if I need to, in order to make this right," Josh said as he made his way toward the door, leaving a stunned Bill in his wake. He decided not to look back because he knew if he did, he might start to have second thoughts.

~

Josh made what was usually a 50 minute drive in 39 minutes and slid into a seat in the bleachers next to a pretty blonde woman a few years younger than him.

Colleen Reynolds was the soccer mom who brought the oranges at halftime of games. The mother that all teenage boys eventually got teased about because she was so attractive. The wife that made Josh the envy of all his friends, and even a few enemies. Colleen was a sweetheart, but like all good mothers, someone who was fiercely protective of her son.

"Didn't think you were going to make it," she said.

"Yeah, I had to walk out in the middle of a meeting and drive 120 miles an hour on the Merritt in order *to* get here, but I wouldn't have missed it."

"He's been looking into the stands every couple of minutes for you."

Almost on cue, Timmy Reynolds looked up, broke into a wide smile and waved to his father. It suddenly made the nerve-wracking drive and his job uncertainty completely worthwhile.

"Little boys and their fathers," Colleen smiled. "He lights up every time you walk into a room."

"Give it a couple of years and he'll be giving me the finger and telling me I'm an a-hole," Josh answered. "By the way, I hope you're well-stocked in feminine products, because I don't think we're going to be getting any more free samples any time soon."

Thirty-two text messages and four phone calls from Pete later, and they finally had a new slogan. He missed a few minutes of the game, but at least he was there. Later that night, he entered his son's dimly lit room to tuck him in and sat down on one corner of the bed.

"Night, pal," Josh said. "You played a great game today."

"Thanks for comin, dad," Timmy answered, before adding what was really on his mind. "You're not going to get fired, are you?"

"Of course not. Why do you ask?"

"Because mom said you left an important meeting to come to my game."

"I'll be ok. Besides, like my dad used to say, 'Family first, last, and in between,'" Josh said as he stood in the doorway. "Night, pal."

"What was he like?" Timmy asked.

"What was who like? My dad?" Josh responded, a bit surprised by the question.

It was something that had been on Timmy's mind for a while. His grandfather had passed away before he had been born, but since his dad rarely spoke of him, he hadn't before mustered the courage to ask.

"Yeah."

"He was…" Josh reflected, "Complicated. But he was a good man."

Josh nodded. He seemed pleased with himself that he had found the right word to describe him.

"Did he used to go to your games?"

"Yes. But I didn't know it at the time."

"How come?"

"It's kind of a long story, pal."

"I'm not very tired," Timmy reasoned.

Josh mulled it over. Decided there was no time like the present. After a slight pause, he began, "My dad…..was smart. He was athletic. Funny. Charming. Beautiful women fell all over him."

"How do you know that?"

"He got your grandmother to marry him, didn't he?"

"No offense, dad, but grandma's old — and wrinkly."

Josh chuckled, "Well, she wasn't always. When your grandmother was younger, everyone thought she was gorgeous."

"Tell me more about your dad," Timmy urged.

"I'll tell you about him on two conditions. One. You keep it between you and I. Not even your mother or grandmother know some of the things I'm about to tell you. And two. If your mother walks in, you shut your eyes and pretend to be asleep so she doesn't yell at me for keeping you up past your bedtime. Deal?"

"Deal," Timmy assured him as he sat up in bed waiting for the story to begin.

"Ok, then. It was my 12th birthday...."